Brilliant

Brilliant

A NOVELLA

GALE SEARS

MEADOW LARK PUBLISHING

For information contact:
gsears1@msn.com
galesears.com

Published by:
Meadow Lark Publishing

Cover and interior book design by
Francine Platt, Eden Graphics, Inc.

Paperback ISBN 979-8-89454-056-6

eBook ISBN 979-8-89454-057-3

Library of Congress Control Number: 2025907040

Manufactured in the United States of America
First Edition

This work is dedicated to my daughter Chandler—
a spark of brilliance that shines in my life.

ACKNOWLEDGMENTS

I gratefully acknowledge my alpha, cultural, and sensitivity readers:
Cindy Pearson, Sabine Berlin, Chris Bond, Teri Boldt, Cynthia
Connell, Kendra Richard, Renee Pay, and Frances Wong.

Also, thank you to my editor, Debbie Rasmussen,
for helping me navigate new territory.

And, always and forever, my husband George.
His encouragement is vital.

One

My first word was debated. Finn dismissed it as babbling or maybe the word, "Bubble." He wasn't really interested in my verbal progress.

Sierra said, "It was definitely Baba." The Hindi name for Grandfather.

I was five months old, so I don't remember. I do remember when I was eight months—standing in my rickety crib and calling for Sierra, frightened of the specters on the shadowed wall.

I will soon be twenty and I have come to watch those walls come down.

The bulldozer from Seattle Construction Company is about to demolish the house of my childhood and I wait for the first blast to penetrate the bedroom where they slept, the front room covered in political posters, and the hardly used kitchen. Maybe the whole thing will go down at once—a flimsy house of cards—kings and queens and mathematics all at once.

"Hey miss! I need you to stand across the street."

"But I want to be close."

"Sorry, not safe. Over there or nowhere." The man thrusts his thumb over his shoulder directing me across the street.

I glance at him. He has small dark eyes and a large nose—the face of Ganesha, elephant god of wisdom and luck.

I nod. One does not argue with a god. I watch my feet as they move across the deserted street. I sit on the bus bench.

Better anyway. Now I'm just a casual observer of the memories.

Baby steps across posters filled with blotches of red. Red flags. Black flags. People walking in and out of the house, noise and clutter.

"Sierra, keep her off the posters!" Finn shouts.

Sierra snaps her fingers at me. "Paige, come here. I have Mr. Ganesha. Come. Come."

I cross the room; hands reaching for my elephant toy. My socks slide on the slick posterboard, and I fall.

"I swear, if she ruins that!"

Sierra scoops me up and I squirm. "It's fine Finn. She didn't damage anything." She puts me on the rug and hands me my elephant.

"Ganesha is hungry," I inform her.

"He's hungry, is he?" She hesitates. "I think I have a banana."

I nod. "Ganesha likes sweet food."

Sierra smiles. "Banana it is. Would you like some too?"

"I will share with him."

Sierra moves to the kitchen, muttering and laughing.

I stand in the doorframe to the front room and watch a

man painting a word on a poster.

"Red."

He looks up and stares at me. I put Ganesha in front of my eyes. "She knows her colors?"

Finn shrugs.

"Man, that kinda freaks me out." He goes back to painting. "And she's not even eighteen months and talking in sentences?"

Finn shrugs again.

"My kid's two and just points at stuff and grunts."

The man and Finn laugh.

The rusted claw slams down on the porch. The support posts buckle and splinters fly everywhere, a portion of the roof crumpling into debris and dust.

I cover my ears and wish for a moment of quiet, but the bulldozer will not stop. It has a job. Its backward crawl is accompanied by loud beeping, then the claw plows into the front wall, shattering the grimy picture window. It grabs the window frame and yanks it forward. The front of the house collapses and I see Sierra in the front room standing as though in meditation. Soon Kali, Hindu goddess of destruction, will come with her red tongue and wide mouth and devour the female sacrifice. I stamp my black flats and I feel a scream snake into my brain.

I stand. I shouldn't have come. I needed to see it go down. I thought I could watch.

"Here, Paige, I'm putting these glow stars and planets on your ceiling. They are magic. They'll keep away the shadows."

I am a stone as the claw chews into the roof. Suddenly, I scream and run into the demolition zone. "Stop! Stop! Someone is in there!"

The man with the face of Ganesha shoves me hard in the chest, knocks the wind out of me, and I fall back. He signals the machine to stop, then turns to me.

I look up at him and struggle for breath. "Someone…in the house."

"Huh? You're nuts. We've checked it a dozen times."

It hurts my chest to talk. "Sierra…she's in there."

The man looks puzzled, "Who?"

"Sierra."

"There's nobody in that house. I went through it two minutes before we started cracking stuff."

A tear slides unwillingly down my cheek.

He offers his hand, but I shake my head.

"You, okay?" he asks.

I rub my chest and struggle to my feet.

"I needed to shove you to keep you from going in there. You know that, right?"

I nod.

"You see anybody in there now?"

I look at the crumbling house. "No."

"Course not. Figment of your imagination."

"But I…"

He yells over me, "Crank it up, George!"

As the claw moves towards the roof, he turns back to me. "So, if you're gonna watch, get back over where it's safe."

I shake my head. I'm done watching. I don't go back to the bus bench. I turn towards the ocean and watch my black flats move along the sidewalk.

As the machine creeps towards the house, I stop and turn back for a final look. The house is an empty cavern and Sierra an uncertain shadow.

The claw smashes the faded asphalt roof, again and again. The magic glow stars and planets don't stand a chance. The dust and dark will eat them.

I cover my ears walk away.

Two

INEGOTIATE THE ROUTE from the bus stop to the college, to the classroom. Thirteen minutes, I now calculate the route to my office, five minutes. I turn the key in the lock. I'm counting to myself before going in when someone approaches.

"Professor Jha?"

I look quickly to my shoes. "Yes?'

"Sorry, didn't mean to give you a fright. Getting the lay of the land, I see."

"Yes, President Nowell. I'm setting my timings."

"I see. Good idea."

"Thank you."

"Are reporters leaving you alone, now that the initial excitement is over?"

I think of pencils, and notebooks, and cameras. "I'm sorry, President Nowell. They were a nuisance when they came on campus."

"Nonsense. They wanted to catch you in your college surroundings. It boosted our exposure, which is always good for the numbers, right?"

"Hmm." I tap my fingers on the door handle.

He raises his eyebrows. "Are you nervous, Professor?"

I glance at his face. "About?"

He chuckles, "Your first day of school?"

"Hmm. I don't think so. I just don't want to be late."

"Indeed. Might set a bad example for your students." He chuckles again. "Well, let me know if you need anything."

Anything?

He walks away and I go into my office. I take a deep breath and turn on the light. I am comforted by my books arranged neatly on the bookshelves, the statue of the Happy Buddha, and my own desk. I run my hand over the smooth surface and think about the cracking of wood—the claw eating into my childhood home.

I clench my fingers into a fist as I imagine images of splintering wood and shattering glass. Dust, dust and disintegrating memories.

Why was Sierra in the house when the roof came down?

I turn to focus on my books, and the statue of Buddha. I reach for him.

"She wasn't there." I speak the words aloud to give them validity. "They would have found her body in the rubble. They would have come to tell Baba that his daughter was dead," I ramble on. "There would have been a story on the seven o'clock news. The workmen would have been questioned. She wasn't there, Paige. She wasn't there."

My phone chortles. It seems to be laughing at my confusion.

"Hello?" It is my grandfather. I take a breath. "Yes. I'm in my office."

I close my eyes and listen to the low rumble of his voice. It calms me.

"Thirteen minutes. The bus stop is at the edge of campus."

I set down the Buddha statue and explain my return route home. "I'm going to get my papers ready for tomorrow, then I will pick up lemons, cinnamon, and chaat masala at the store, and then take the bus home."

I sigh. "Yes, Baba. I will live my life well."

I shut down my phone. and look out my office window. *She wasn't there.*

Three

TIME. *Time again. Check the power point. Don't mind the chatter. Begin.*

"Good morning. This is Far Eastern philosophy. Philosophy 110, a three-credit class. We will use three textbooks: *Tao Te Ching* by Lao Tzu, *The Analects of Confucius*, and *Looking into the Sun*. You should have read the introduction to *Looking into the Sun*, prior to this first class. If you have not read…"

"Professor Jha?"

A young woman in the third row has her hand in the air.

"Yes?"

"You wrote, *Looking into the Sun?*"

"Yes. In collaboration."

"When you were how old?"

"Sixteen. What's your name?"

"Sierra."

"Excuse me?"

"Sierra Wheeler."

"Oh." I clench my pen.

Click, click, click.

"Is something wrong, Professor?"

"It's just that I know someone else named Sierra—*another* Sierra." I feel like a page torn out of a book as my mind shifts.

I kick my toes on the shoebox, stopping when Finn hisses at me. "Just read."

Another dollar drops into the shoebox.

A pair of red shoes stops beside Finn. "Did you train her to do that?"

"Do what? She's reading."

"Right. How old is she, five?"

"Four."

"And she's reading that?"

"Yeah. Narnia... something. She likes it." Finn looks at me. "So, get on with it, Einstein."

I take a breath and read. "And the deck and the sail and their own faces and bodies became brighter and brighter and even the rope shone. And the next morning, when the sun rose, now five or six times its old size, they stared hard into it and could see the very feathers of the birds that came flying from it."

The red shoes are at the box.

"She's obviously memorized it."

"Yeah? Well, even that would be amazing, right? So why don't you pull a bill outta your expensive Gucci bag and give it to her?"

"That was rude."

"Ruder than you calling my kid a fraud or a trained monkey?"

"She can read anything?"

"She can. And, if she reads whatever you give her, you throw twenty bucks in the box."

"Safe bet." From the Gucci comes a piece of paper. "Here, have her read this."

"Okay P, let's take the nice lady's money."

"Eggs, bowtie pasta, apples, asparagus, 2% milk, unsalted butter, six croissants…"

"I…what…how?"

Finn laughs loudly. "Man, you should see your face." He glares at her and clicks his fingers. "Remember, she needs new shoes."

"She should be in a special school."

"Haven't found one special enough, but we'll keep trying. So?"

Twenty bucks falls into the shoebox. She pats my head. "Precious little girl."

"Precious: of great value, not to be wasted or treated carelessly," I state.

The red shoes walk away, and I want to follow. Finn picks up the shoebox, takes the money and shoves it into the pocket of his faded jeans. The box goes into the backpack.

"Hand me the book." I disobey. He flips my forehead. "Come on, give it." I do. He glances in the direction of the red shoes. "Capitalist tramp."

Ganesha and I step back.

"Hey! Where you going?"

I step back three more steps.

"Get over here. We have to find Sierra."

I watch my feet as they go forward, moving like the wind-up doll I saw at Filbert's Department store corner of Main and Crocker. $37.99 plus tax.

"Buy now! Almost out of stock!"

Finn yanks my braid. "What's up?"

"Buy now! Almost out of stock!"

He bumps my back with the backpack. "Get a move on. And quit talking that bourgeois crap."

"Bourgeois: the bourgeoisie revolutionized industry and brought on the modern society. But it also exploited the proletariat. Workers of the world unite!"

"Hush, P."

"Workers of the world unite!"

"Hush up, now! And put your fist down. People are gonna think you're crazy." He shoves my hand down and I shake off his touch.

"Crap."

"Paige, shut up."

"Bourgeois crap. Crap: something of extremely poor quality. Nonsense. Rubbish. Crap: excrement."

"Hey!" a voice calls out. "Don't let her use that language."

"Get lost, mister." Finn laughs and bumps me with the backpack. "You're gonna get me in trouble you keep that up. He laughs again. "Revolutionary punk."

"Revolutionary punk." I mumble.

"Let's find Sierra."

"I'm hungry."

"Well, maybe she's found some food. She's good at play-ing miserable."

"Miserable, despondent, wretched, regretful, broken-hearted."

A slap on my head. I touch the place where the lady with the red shoes patted me. Ganesha and I struggle to keep up with Finn—it's hard, but we must. He has my books in his backpack.

"Professor Jah?" A voice calls out.

"The…the relevant issue is your reading." There is a sweep of muted laughter. I pick up my pen.

Click, click, click

It calms me.

"If you have not read the introduction to *Looking into the Sun*, you are behind." I lay my pen perpendicular to the right edge of the podium. "We will begin our journey into Eastern philosophy with the creation story of Hinduism, in which a beginning does not exist."

Four

"Professor, Jha?"

"Yes?"

"I'm in this class—physics 105."

"Yes. Your name?"

"Kennedy. You assigned us that book by Margaret Jeller."

Unconsciously, I picked up my pen.

Click, click, click

"Thesis." I stare at her mouth. She has a metal stud in her lower lip.

"Huh?"

"Not book. Thesis. Her thesis. And it's Geller not Jeller."

"Ah, okay. I didn't quite catch the title—Bright Galaxies in something?"

"Bright Galaxies in Rich Clusters: A Statistical Model for Magnitude Distributions."

"Ah, okay. Can I find it under the first part?"

I resist the urge to click my pen. "I assume. Why don't you try?"

Kennedy glares at me. "Isn't it your job to help?"

I don't respond—transfixed by the metal in her lip.

"What are you staring at, Professor?"

"That stud in your lower lip. It looks painful."

Kennedy's lips press together, and I wince. My eyes flick to her face—*her* eyes narrow.

"My friends warned me about taking this class," she growls.

I step back.

"They said you're weird, and you come from a weird family."

I watch Sierra dancing in the star strewn night, head back, fingertips reaching for the Butterfly Nebula. I see her dancing, but she is muted: brown flannel shirt, long brown hair, brown eyes—all disappearing as she dances in the darkness. They dance with her—the Flaming Star, the Blue Flash, the Little Ghost Nebula. I want to join but my long brown hair is braided, and I don't know how to dance.

The bell rings and Kennedy stomps back to her seat. I glance around the lecture hall at my twenty-four students. Some are talking with their peers, some drinking coffee, and some looking directly at me, apparently intrigued by my interaction with Kennedy. I pick up a paper and display it.

"Good morning, class." My voice is soft and shaky. "You will find in front of you, mandalas."

The talking continues.

The first day in the lecture hall no one took notice of me as I stood at the front removing papers from my computer bag. When I addressed them, several thought I was the teachers aid.

I take a deep breath and speak firmly as my grandfather coached me. "I will begin the lecture now."

The class quiets.

"You will find in front of you, mandalas. A mandala is a geometric figure representing the universe in Hindu and Buddhist symbolism. You may wonder what this has to do with physics. I will explain the mathematics of the universe after you finish coloring. I assigned you to bring colored pencils."

A few moans from the forgetful.

"If you have not, perhaps you can ask a classmate to share. You will have half the class to color, after which we will discuss sacred symbols, mathematical oneness, and the search for completeness and self-unity."

I knock on the door with a plaque. Dr. Jacob Lee.

"Come in."

I adjust the shoulder strap on my book bag. I open the door, count to four, and step inside.

"Ah, Paige! Come in! Come in!"

"You asked to see me, Dr. Lee?"

"Yes, have a seat." He holds the back of the chair for me. I place my book bag on the floor and sit. As he moves back to his chair, I notice a new carving on the wall. It is a Lotus Flower.

"A new carving."

"Yes." He swivels in his chair. "Eighteenth century. What do you think?" He turns to face me and his eyes crinkle at the corners as he smiles.

"Hmm." I try to assess if he is happy or proud. "You like it."

"I do."

I nod. "The sacred lotus flower is an object of great power symbolizing the ultimate purity of mind and heart."

"And why?" he asks.

"Because it rises untainted and beautiful from the mud," I pause. "Was it expensive?"

He chuckles. "Even your grandfather would not have the nerve to ask me that, and we have been friends thirty-five years."

"Thirty-six."

"Indeed." Dr. Lee leans forward, and I look at my book-bag. "So, Professor Jha, the reason for our meeting."

I sit up straight. It's uncomfortable.

"I want to know how you feel about your first week as a teacher?"

I'm thinking, *How do I feel?* "I don't think they understand me."

"You or the subject matter?"

"Ummm, both."

"Their first exam will show their grasp of the subject matter, correct?"

I nod again.

"And, as for you?" He waits, studying me.

"They find me odd."

"You have always had to deal with being unique, Paige. So, what is different in this situation?"

"I am their same age. Why would they trust me to teach them?"

"Gaining a student's trust is the same for every teacher. The young upstarts come into the classroom ready to challenge everything you say—ready to find fault."

"Not with you."

"Well, I've been teaching for thirty years. I have a reputation."

"The Chinese Dragon."

Dr. Lee laughs loudly and I cover my ears.

"Sorry, Paige. Sorry. You just disarmed me with your candor."

I glance at him. He continues to chuckle and shake his head. "The Chinese Dragon," he mumbles. After a moment of silence, "Dr. Jha…" His tone is different. "Have you talked with your students about your spectrum?"

I look at the Lotus Flower carving. "No."

"I think it would help if you did."

I sit still, silent.

"Paige, look at me. I know it's difficult, but I need you to see me."

I look. I have known him for eight years and three months, so it is easier to look at his face than most. He is my grandfather's friend. He knew my grandmother before she died. He knew Sierra. I *do* see him. "Hmm."

"Remember when we were in our meeting with President Nowell and the committee?"

"When I was hired."

"Yes. I suggested then that you explain your eccentricities to your students, and the committee agreed."

"Hmm."

"Be straight with your students. Tell them about your spectrum. They'll get it. Better than the whispered gossip and conjecture."

"Hmm."

"Your grandfather agrees with me."

I turn back to the Lotus Flower.

"As your mentor, I'm asking you think about it."

I nod.

I think about everything.

"Okay. Good." He rolls an orange across his desk to me. I poke it to make it stop. "Now…has your grandfather spoken to you about your appearance?"

I take my eyes off the orange and look at him. "My appearance?"

"Obviously not, so I will take it up." He leans forward even further. "Professor Jha, why do you always wear long skirts and sweaters to school?"

I tug at the hem of my cardigan. "They're comfortable."

"And the Birkenstocks?"

"Comfortable." I begin to peel the orange. "Am I not supposed to wear things that are comfortable?"

He grins. "There's nothing's wrong with being comfortable; I'm just suggesting that up-to-date clothing would make you look more like a teacher and less like a student. Isn't that what you want?"

"Yes." I continue peeling my orange. "Should I cut my hair?"

"Heaven's no. Your long braid speaks of your culture."

"Then I should wear a sari."

Dr. Lee flops back into his chair. "I think I've put myself in a corner."

"Your chair is in the middle of the room, Dr. Lee."

He flicks his hands at me. "Never mind. Never mind. I will take it up with Avi."

"My grandfather doesn't know fashion."

Dr. Lee groans. "Let's change the subject."

"Hmm."

"I want to know about the other faculty members?"

"What about them?"

"Do they speak with you?"

"About what?" I finish peeling the orange.

"Dr. Jha, are you being intentionally obtuse?"

"No, I'm not. I just don't know them. We haven't spoken."

He sighs. "You may want to change that."

"Why? Is it required for my work here?"

Dr. Lee takes a deep breath and shakes his head. "No, not required, but I think it will make your job more enjoyable."

"How?"

"You have risen from the mud, Paige Jha!"

His voice booms and I drop my orange peelings to the floor.

"You have risen up a remarkable lotus flower from the mud. You must now look and see that there are other beautiful lotus flowers around you."

"And mud."

"Yes, yes. And mud. But, let the flowers catch your eye." His voice softens. "You are a wonder, Paige. A wonder. And, even within your spectrum you are unique. The neuroscientists don't know what to make of you."

"Hmm."

"You deal with a spectrum that attempts to isolate you, yet you choose to push out of your isolation—you choose to be a teacher, not a quantum physicist, not a mathematician, not a scholar. A teacher. A profession where the entire purpose is to disseminate facts and ideas and connect with other human beings. To make them think." He taps his temple several times and takes another deep breath. "Why? Why did you choose teaching?"

I'm four, and I'm reading a Buddhist children's story to Ganesha and Sierra—the story of *The Foolish Leopard*. Ganesha asks me if there are Irish Pixies in the story. I say no. He gets upset. I tell him not to stamp around or trumpet. I tell Sierra that she should teach Ganesha meditation. She says she'll try. I shake my finger at the unruly elephant.

"You must listen carefully to the story, Ganesha so that Buddha can teach you."

Sierra smiles at me and calls me a wise teacher.

I read how the leopard is king of his domain. No one questions him or tells him what to do. One day a colorful parrot flies into his jungle and warns him that he must move further south. The leopard snarls at the parrot with his fearsome fangs and it flies away. The next day the parrot returns and warns the leopard again that it must move further south. The leopard swipes at the parrot with his sharp claws and slices her wing. The parrot flies away, wounded and weeping. The next day the parrot does not come, but the hunter comes and captures the tiger and takes him far from his domain.

"Buddha teaches that the wise person should always be willing to learn from others who may see things from a different perspective."

Dr. Lee smiles. "Yes, like I said, to make them think."

I look into his eyes. "Sometimes they say 'awesome.'"

"I beg your pardon?"

"Awesome. Sometimes I tell them something and I hear voices from the class members saying 'awesome.'"

A bigger smile spreads across Professor Lee's face. "Yes. It's a good word. A teacher likes the sound of awesome."

There is a knock on the office door and Dr. Lee stands. "Ah, that is my three-thirty consultation."

I stand too, then I notice the orange peelings. I stoop to pick them up but it's difficult with my bookbag and my hand full of the fruit. "Sorry, I made a mess." I turn to set the orange on his desk.

"Never mind, Professor Jha," he says, coming next to me. "I'll pick it up."

I don't move, but stare at the orange sitting on my flat palm. "I…"

Dr. Lee takes it from my hand. "Too much to navigate."

"Hmm. Thank you.

Another knock.

"Yes! I'll be with you in a moment."

"Oh! Oh, okay. Sorry," comes a male voice from the other side of the door.

Dr. Lee chuckles. "I think he's afraid of the Chinese Dragon."

I try to mimic his smile. "I think he is."

I pick up my computer bag and Dr. Lee escorts me to the door. "Now, there is a faculty luncheon next Friday. I think we should attend."

"Hmm."

"I will pick you up at your office at noon on that day."

"But I…"

"It will make your job more enjoyable." He opens the door for his next appointment—a wide-eyed young man with a tee shirt that says Dave Matthew's Band. "Mr. Kimball! Come in."

I know him. A student in my physics class. He looks surprised to see me.

"Professor Jha?"

"Mr. Kimball."

I glance up at him as he moves through the doorframe—
he slightly ducks his head. I stop at the door, count to four,
and step into the hallway. I don't look back but I call to Dr
Lee. "Thank you. I will think about the luncheon."

"Awesome!"

He closes the door.

Perhaps Dr. Lee is the parrot, and I am the leopard.

Five

I TURN THE KEY in the lock, place my hand on the doorknob, and open the door. I count to four and enter. I breathe deeply—the smell of cinnamon and bay leaf. Atikka stew.

Grandfather is cooking.

I place my keys in the blue ceramic bowl on the entry way table, my book bag on the wall peg, and my briefcase on the floor by the umbrella stand. I adjust the picture of grandmother and say good evening to her.

"Professor Jha?" comes a voice from the kitchen. "Are you home?"

"I am home, Baba."

I walk down the hall, past the living room to the kitchen. My grandfather stands at the stove sizzling cumin in ghee. He turns to me and beams. I have memorized that expression. It's one he often uses when he looks at me.

He removes the pan from the hot burner.

"So, your first week is complete."

I nod.

"And what are you thinking?"

This is a difficult question. Not as difficult as what are you feeling, but still…difficult. I watch him stirring the spice. "I think I'll stay."

Another broad smile. "Wonderful! So, this celebration dinner will not go to waste."

"Celebration? Why?"

"Your first week of teaching—done, finished, completed!"

"There are many weeks to go."

"So be it. But this is a banner event. Youngest professor in the nation finishes her first week without jumping ship." He brings the pan to his face and breaths deeply. "Yes. We are going to celebrate."

"Associate professor," I remind him.

"You'll have your PHD in six months."

"And I would never jump from a ship. I can't swim."

Baba's eyes narrow. "Are you going to stand here arguing with me, Little Twig, or go change clothes and help me with the Naan bread?"

"Change clothes."

"Good. Because Aakesh and Elly are coming and also Dr. Lee."

I stop and turn back. "I met with him today. He didn't mention coming."

"I told them to wait until I found out if you were okay with it."

"Hmm." I consider. I am comfortable with Aakesh and Elly.

My uncle is eight years younger than Sierra and came to

our house once to announce his and Elly's engagement. I was eleven and fascinated by Elly's blue eyes and pale skin. She also wore make-up, which Sierra avoided except to hide bruises. I stared at Elly when she wasn't looking in my direction.

"We brought Paige a Seahawks sweatshirt," Uncle Aakesh says, handing me a package.
"We don't need handouts," Finn says.
"It's not a handout—it's a gift." Elly intervenes.
"And who says she wants it?"
I hug the package. "I want it."

"I want a celebration dinner, Baba. Besides, everyone needs to come because you're making a lot of food."
Baba salutes me with the wooden spoon. "I will call and let them know. Hurry back to help."

After dinner, Elly plays songs on the piano. Easy soft music. Barry Manilow. Dr. Lee wanted me to play Chopin, but I wanted to listen. I curl in the recliner under one of grandmother's crocheted blankets, as heaviness presses in. I hear Elly's music but other tones drift into my mind— childhood music. Dadi teaching me the notes.

I play the music on the paper. My fingers stretch to press the keys. My Dadi sits in the rocker under a crocheted blanket; her finger taps the time on the arm of the chair. I stop playing because I hear Sierra and Grand-father's loud voices from the back porch. Grandfather's voice is pleading. Sierra's voice is angry. Dadi scolds me.

"Never stop the song in the middle, Paige. You must always play to the end."

I play the notes from where I stopped. I play to the end. I look at Dadi and she nods. I begin the song again. Sierra comes in and tells me it's time to go. I tell her I have to play to the end of the song. She grabs my wrist and I pull away.

"No! I have to play to the end! Dadi says I must play to the end!"

I begin to play faster. Whenever Sierra reaches for me, I push at her arm and play faster—faster, and faster until the end. I lay my head on the keys. Sierra picks me up and heads for the door. I squirm to be put down but she squeezes me tighter. When I look back, I see Dadi's gaze fixed on my face and her hands in the namaste prayer.

The men stop talking and clap for Elly's performance. She has come to the end of the song. She stands, attempts a little bow, and then stretches her back. Her baby is due in two months. They will name him Yash Edmond Jha; Edmond for Elly's father and Yash which, in Hindi, means majesty.

I clap for Elly's performance and think about the birth of Yash Jha—jealous that Sierra neglected to give me an Indian name.

Six

"MAN'S VIEWS ARE FINITE. We think in terms of beginnings and endings. The idea of an infinite construct frightens us. We grasp for meaning. It's the same with science and the universe, science must start with a beginning."

"The Big Bang theory," a student calls out.

I find the face. Brown curly hair. Hazel eyes. Mr. Kimball and the Dave Matthews Band.

"Yes, Mr. Kimball. The Big Bang theory." He seems pleased that I said his name.

I draw a circle on the white board and scribble in a few rough continents. "This is an accurate representation of the earth."

The class chuckles. Baba said they would. I place a dot somewhere in the United States. "And this is you. This is not an accurate representation. If it were, you would be about the size of Los Angeles."

The class laughs and I feel molecules tumbling through the air. "And out there…" I motion everywhere. "Is the vast universe and beyond."

A young man with glasses calls out, "To infinity and beyond!"

"Yes, Mr. Isakson. And beyond and beyond and beyond."

I point at the dot on the map. "So, here we are, these little specks, trying to make sense of the universe." I bring up an image of an ocean on the power point. "Sir Isaac Newton surmised that what we know is a drop—what we don't know is an ocean. I agree with him. I believe that science is relentless skepticism."

A hand shoots into the air. "Yes?"

"Skepticism?"

"Yes."

"I disagree. Science deals with facts."

I clutch my pen.

Click, click, click

"Your name is Kennedy, correct?"

"Kennedy Everett. And science is science."

"It's an interesting idea Kennedy, but what does it mean, science is science? Has science never altered its views?"

"Not about things like gravity."

"That would be news to Tessa Baker."

"Who's that?"

"She's a cosmologist at Queen Mary University in London."

"So?"

"I will leave you to find her online and read about what she and her colleagues are discovering about dark energy."

"Whatever."

Click click click.

I am eight and Finn and Sierra are fighting. She wants to go home and see grandmother who is sick. He says that the revolution requires us to give up our parents with their old customs and old thinking. She accuses him that he hasn't given up his parents. He says because they are revolutionaries who taught him about the struggle. With tears, Sierra says her mother taught her to play the piano.

"I want to go see Dadi."

Finn glares at me. "You stay out of this. It's none of your business."

"Dadi is part of my business. She taught me to play the piano too."

Sierra grabs his arm as he goes for me. "Paige don't talk back," she begs.

"Are you arguing with me, misfit?"

"The superior man is satisfied and composed; the common man is always full of distress."

"Paige!" Sierra shrieks.

I step back.

"Go to your room! Go on now. Go find Ganesha and read him a story."

I go to my room, shut the door, and press my hands over my ears.

"A teacher should teach you *how* to think, not *what* to think. What to think, with no questioning, is indoctrination. Theory is the supposition—a system of ideas intended to explain something. Every good scientist tests the theory. I will give you facts and opinions, which you'll need to test and measure. I want you to test and measure everything you're told."

Kennedy sneers, "So, everything you say I can question?" Her words are clipped—the voice of a petulant five-year-old.

"Test and measure. Yes. But you need to be sincere and open-minded in your questioning."

"What does that mean?"

"After investigation, you should be willing to admit if your original belief or theory was lacking or incorrect."

"Why?"

Some of the other students begin to murmur and shift in their seats.

Mr. Kimball challenges, "What's your problem, Kennedy?"

"No problem. I just thought we were supposed to come here for the answers. My Dad's paying a butt load of money for me to be here and learn something, yet she's saying I need to test and measure." Kennedy's bitter voice is confrontational. "Then what are we paying her for?"

I reach in my pocket.

Click click click.

I put my pen perpendicular on the right edge of the podium and walk to the front. "So, I have a question."

The class settles, but Kennedy glares at me.

"What came before the Big Bang?"

Silence.

"Before?" someone asks.

"Yes, before."

Silence.

"So, why don't you earn your pay and teach us something?" Kennedy challenges.

I take a deep breath. "The most brilliant cosmologists, physicists, and astrophysicists have no idea what came before."

Silence.

"In the beginning was the Word and the Word was with God, and the Word was God." Mister Kimball quotes.

"Hey!" Kennedy shouts.

"The same was in the beginning with God."

Kennedy jumps to her feet. "Hey! Shut up! You can't preach that crap in class."

Mr. Kimball continues. "And all things were made by him; and without him was not anything made that was made."

Kennedy points at me. "You can't let him say that stuff in class!"

"Can Mr. Kimball not state his views?"

"No. Separation of Church and State."

"I don't think that means what you think it does, Miss Everett."

"Don't Miss Everett me. You're my same age." She grabs her bag and mumbles, "What a freak."

"Hey!" Mr. Kimball shouts. "You can't talk to a teacher that way!"

"And you can't talk your revolting Jesus talk." She shoves past the students in her row and stops in the isle. "I'm going to report this." She gives me a hateful look. "Teacher? You're not a teacher. You're a joke. You're supposed to have this big brain, but you don't even know how to run your class. Conservative freak."

Mr. Kimball shoves his chair back and stands. "What's the matter with you?"

Kennedy glares at him. "Nothing's the matter with me. I just can't stand the crap she's trying to shove down our throats."

I step back and cover my ears to block out her snarling voice, and the stomp of her thick soled boots as she ascends the stairs.

"Science is science! Science is science! Science is science!" she yells, like she's at a protest rally.

I glance at the class—dozens of eyes stare at me. My hands drop to my sides. "Class dismissed."

I wander over to turn off the power point keeping my back to the students as they exit. The classroom is quiet now. I close my eyes and think of wind blowing through a stand of bamboo.

"Professor Jha?" Mr. Kimball's soft voice comes from behind me. "I'm sorry. I had no idea…"

I nod and slowly close the lid to my computer, then everything goes dark.

I sit on Dadi's bed as Sierra plays Chopin. *Piano concerto #1 in E minor*. Dadi's thin arms lie on top of the coverlet. I look at her hands once busy with making flatbread and guiding me at the piano. Her fingers are still—no tapping of the time. She has come to the end of the song.

"Dadi?"

Her breath is ragged, but her eyes open. "Yes, Jaanu?"

The Hindi word for beloved touches my ear like a prayer.

"Do you want to be reincarnated or live in heaven?"

Her words are slow in coming. "These are deep thoughts, Paige Jha. Why do you ask this?"

I trace the veins on the back of her hand. "I want to know where to find you."

A sound like the mewling of a small kitten escapes her throat. She closes her eyes. "I choose Heaven."

"Paige! Paige Jha!" Someone is pinching the back of my hand. "Professor Jha, wake up!"

There is light on my eyelids and pain in my elbow. I open my eyes and look into the face of Dr. Lee.

"What?"

"You fainted. Thanks to Mr. Kimball, you didn't crack your head."

"Fainted?"

With Dr. Lee's help, I slowly sit up and catch a glimpse of Mr. Kimball hovering by the podium.

"Why are you here, Dr. Lee?"

"Mr. Kimball caught me in the hallway."

I glance at him, and he smiles.

Dr. Lee pats my back. "What happened?"

"It was too loud and there was tension."

"Tension? Why?"

I rub my temples, unable to put the feelings into words.

Mr. Kimball speaks up. "A girl in our class was being a jerk. She took offence at something Professor Jha said, and she just wouldn't shut up about it."

"Oh, dear."

"She got loud and obnoxious. I'm afraid I didn't help."

"How's that?"

"I started quoting bible verses to her."

Dr. Lee chuckles. "Well, that's generally a fire starter."

"Yes, professor. Sorry."

"Not your fault."

"She doesn't like me." I start to get up. Dr. Lee puts a hand on my shoulder.

"Sit still, Paige. The campus medical will be here in a minute."

"No! No-no-no." I stand too quickly and sway.

Mr. Kimball is immediately by my side, a hand on my waist. I take a breath and maneuver around him, hurriedly putting away my papers and computer.

"Paige, you need to wait for them," Dr. Lee instructs.

"No. I can't. Mr. Kimball caught me. I didn't crack my head. I'm fine." I gather my bags and head for the stairs.

"Paige, they need to make a report."

I ignore him.

"Paige!"

"Tell them I'm fine!" I count to four and push through the door into the deserted hallway. I move against the wall and hide my face as two red-vested medics rush past.

Outside the building I meet with a Seattle drizzle. I open my umbrella and walk quickly towards my office sanctuary. The word *freak* follows me.

Seven

I HAVE MEMORIES of kicking through the crunchy red, yellow and brown leaves, and smelling the wet earth. Sierra would sneak me to Baba and Dadi's house just to kick the leaves. I would ask for them, but Sierra would tap my nose, mumble, and tell me they were out running errands. She would kick the leaves with me, and I would see a different face.

Now I gather leaves with Baba, Dadi has gone to heaven, Sierra is missing, and I am a teacher.

My metal rake stutters against the ground as it collects the golden maple leaves. Baba planted the tree when Sierra was five. The family came from India and moved onto Marine View Drive. I lift my rake and see that leaves are stuck between the metal tongs. I reach to release them. I would prefer the wooden rake but since it is Baba's favorite I don't complain. It's good to be outside with a cool breeze on my face. It's good to be away from the classroom.

"Where are you, Paige Jha?" Grandfather asks me.

"In the yard, raking. I am ten feet from you, Baba."

He chuckles. "Yes, but where are you in your thoughts?"

"Hmm." I scoop a large gob of leaves onto the pile. "I am in India, and here raking, and at the college."

"Still thinking of the noisy belligerent student?"

"Hmm."

He stops working and comes over to me. "Shall we sit on the porch steps for a moment?" He lays his rake down. "I could use a break."

"Hmm." I follow him.

He sits with a grunt. "Getting old."

I don't like these words. "You will live a long time, Baba. You are healthy. No major surgeries. No cancer like Dadi."

"Ah." He holds up the index finger of his right hand which indicates that I should stop talking. "Do not worry Paige Jha. I must stay on earth to help raise Yash Jha."

"Of course, because Aakesh might jumble things."

"Elly will be fine, but Aakesh might indeed jumble things." Baba removes a leaf from my hair. "So, what is troubling you, Little Twig?"

"The girl has reported me to the President."

"As you've told me."

"He's called me in for a meeting on Monday."

"And?"

"He'll ask me why I can't control my class. He'll tell me I shouldn't be a teacher."

"Are you sure of that?"

"Hmm."

Baba shrugs. "Perhaps you shouldn't be a teacher."

"What? Is that what you think?"

"It doesn't matter what I think, it's what you think."

I click my fingers in agitation. "But she was yelling and Mr. Kimball was quoting bible verses…"

"Dastardly." Baba lays his hand on mine. "Paige."

I move away. "I can't even get my students to understand the power of critical thinking."

"One crazy student running off her mouth."

"Baba!"

"What? It's true, isn't it? Besides, it's not your job."

"What?" I lay my hands flat on my thighs. "What's not my job?"

"Getting them to understand. That's their job."

I force myself to breathe. "The President may not see it that way. He'll wonder why I can't control my class."

"Is that what *you* wonder?"

"Of course."

"Paige, it takes time for a teacher to settle into their style."

"Hmm."

Baba presses his palms together, and for a moment I think he might pray. "I am a mathematician. I deal with axioms and postulates."

"Hmm."

"Positive and negative numbers." I glance at his face as a smile curves his lips. "When I was first teaching at the college, there was a nickname which followed me."

"Brahmagupta," I insert quickly.

He winks at me. "Brahmagupta—the finder of negative numbers. And as a young professor I was stern. I thought I had to be like that to earn the student's respect."

"It doesn't fit you."

"How's that?"

"Because you are too positive."

Baba laughs at my joke. "You are always surprising me, Paige Jha."

The blue sky looks bluer. "Hmm."

"But don't get me off topic." Baba touches the back of my hand—the sign that I should pay attention. "It took me a while to find a better style; to be able to efficiently engage the students with humor."

"But I…"

"Paige, give yourself time. I was thirty when I began teaching. You're nineteen."

"I hope President Nowell gives me time."

"Because you want to keep teaching, right?"

"I do."

"So!" Baba says loudly and I jump. "I will tell you a story that might help in your meeting with the President. Perhaps if nothing else, it will give *you* perspective."

"Perspective is useful."

Baba claps his hands. "It is! First, it's important to understand that we are a family of scientists: Aakesh is a scientist of economics, me, math, you physics, while Dadi and your mom studied the science of music."

My eyes narrow at the word "mom."

I sit at the edge of the sandbox avoiding the sand and staring at the domed metal structure in the grassy area.

Triangles.

A boy dangles from one of the bars. He calls over and over one word—mom. Mom. Mom. Mom. His voice becoming shrill. I cover my ears and watch as a person runs to hold him and help him to the ground. He wraps his arms around her legs. When Sierra comes to get me from the sandbox, I say mom. Her eyes are wide. I look at the sand.

"You …you can't call me that, Paige." she says in a whisper. "Finn won't stand for it. Never call me mom, always call me Sierra." She lifts me to my feet and I back away.

I force myself to listen to Baba telling his story. "Once there was a brilliant scientist who lived by his faith in the power of reason. He toiled and struggled all his earthly existence to find the meaning of life. He braved the deserts of deduction, swam the rivers of theory…"

"Baba, you are so dramatic."

"Shh. Don't interrupt my story." He takes a deep breath. "And climbed the mountains of matter and anti-matter!"

I shake my head at his antics but stay silent.

"As an old man he is about to scale the final mountain of ignorance—to conquer the highest peak; as he pulls himself over the final rock…" Baba pauses for dramatic effect. "He is greeted by a band of theologians who have been sitting there for centuries."

I mirror his smile as we ponder deserts, rivers, mountains, and faith. I bring my hands together in a namaste prayer and softly clap. "Like C.S. Lewis."

"Yes. And his friends: Tolkien, and Sir Isaac, and Hubble and…"

"You."

He pulls my braid and stands. "Favored to be in the company of believers." He grabs his rake. "Now, come on you sluggard! Let's get this done before lunch."

I join him. "It is a good story, Baba, but I don't know how this will help me in my meeting."

"If President Nowell loses *his* perspective and begins to chastise you for teaching critical thinking and allowing bible verses to be quoted, you can tell him the story. He likes Jastrow."

"Jastrow?"

"Robert Jastrow—the scientist who created the tale."

"You're a cleaver one, Baba."

"Thank you."

I go back to my raking—thinking of the science of music.

Sierra and Dadi play *The Snow Maiden Act III* by Korsakov while Ganesha and I conduct. Dadi sits at the piano, her carriage straight and poised as her slender fingers find the keys. Sierra sways as her bow makes the violin sing. They play to the end, but the thrum of the last note does not diminish. The note presses against my ears, and I tell Ganesha he must stop conducting or the note will never end. He places a string of marigolds around my neck and reminds me he is the bringer of good fortune.

Baba calls to me, "Paige Jha, you are off in your thoughts again."

"Hmm." I look at him. My eyes narrow as I press my lips together.

"What is that face?"

"Baba, where is Ganesha?"

"I beg your pardon?"

"My Ganesha. Where is he? I remember everything, Baba, but I don't remember where we put Ganesha. Is he lost?"

My grandfather stops raking and stands very still. "I think he must be lost, Paige. I'm sorry."

There is a look on his face which I cannot read. Is it fear?

Eight

"Now, for the end of class I want to go through the Confucian philosophy of the attainment of peace in the world. Where does it begin? Lydia?"

Miss Aston looks up; she seems surprised that I used her first name. "Rightness in the heart."

"Which leads to?"

"Beauty in the character."

"Yes, Miss Aston, thank you. If there is rightness in the heart, there will be beauty in the character."

I bring up an image of Confucius on the power point. "We need to remember that the sage wrote this dialogue sometime during the Warring States Period 475-222 BC, a period of great unrest and geopolitical restructuring." I change the picture to one of an ancient Chinese battle scene.

"Let's continue the dialogue. If there is beauty in the character. Yes, Mr. Wheaten?"

"There will be harmony in the home."

I fade out the battle scene and bring up a painting from the Tang Dynasty of a happy family. "And if there is harmony in the home?"

Several hands fly into the air. "Yes?"

"There will be order in the nation," voices say in unison.

A rumble of laughter from their classmates.

"And Miss Aston if you will bookend the dialogue? If there is order in the nation?"

"There will be peace in the world."

"Yes. Thank you." My power point displays a series of lotus blossoms. "Rightness in the heart...beauty in the character...harmony in the home...order in the nation... peace in the world."

I bring up pictures of kind faces, beautiful landscapes, and happy families, ending with a NASA photo of the earth.

"So, what do we think of this philosophy?"

"Impossible."

"Why is that Mr. Wheaten?"

"How many people do you know with rightness of heart, Professor?"

"What does that even mean?" someone else questions.

A discussion begins concerning the definition of rightness of heart. I stand back and enjoy the exchange, pondering myself—the meaning of rightness of heart.

I sit in a highchair watching Sierra open and close cupboard doors. She uses profanity and I mimic her.

"Paige, don't!"

"Ganesha is hungry."

She slams the cupboard door. "I know!" Softer. "I know."

She finds a box of Rice Chex, shaking it to reveal a few squares still hiding in the bottom. She dumps them onto my tray. I stare at them.

"Fourteen," I count.

"Great. Eat up."

The front door opens, and Finn comes in. He carries a box, and the warm smell of food comes with him into the kitchen.

Sierra stares at him. "Where did you get that?"

"The sponsors bought us pizza after the protest and gave us each fifty bucks."

Sierra rubs her face and drops into a chair at the kitchen table. "Is there milk or anything?"

"Just pizza."

"But Paige can't..."

"She can eat the crust." He grabs some pizza, kisses Sierra on the forehead, and sets a small plastic bottle on the table. Orange—white top. "Stop complaining." He moves out of the kitchen. "I need to watch the news."

Sierra nods and her shaky hand reaches for the orange bottle. I watch her staring at the floor. I eat a Rice Chex.

"Who defines rightness of heart?"

Is someone speaking to me?

"Professor Jha?"

"Yes?"

"Did Confucius define the qualities of a person who has rightness of heart?"

"The sage does give us some guidance here." The bell

rings. "Which we will discuss in our next class."

The students gather their belongings and head out of the classroom, continuing the discussion as they go. I am settled by the rumble of their voices. I turn off my computer and place it in its bag. I put my pen in my satchel along with my notebooks and papers. I walk to the door and take hold of the handle, but the door pulls open from the other side and I am yanked into the hallway.

"Oh!" My mind races. I close my eyes and count to four.

"Sorry, Professor Jha. I was just coming to see you."

I open my eyes and see Mr. Kimball.

"About an assignment?"

He stammers, "Ah…no. I wanted to ask you something."

"Go on then."

"Were you called to meet with President Nowell?"

I begin walking and he accompanies me. "Why would you think that?"

"Because he called me in to ask about the incident with Kennedy."

"Hmm."

"It seems she complained directly to him. I guess her dad's a big doner or something, so he had to look into it."

I don't say anything.

"I was worried that you might be in trouble."

"I am not in trouble."

"Oh, good. That's good. Because Kennedy was totally out of line."

"She has a right to her opinion."

"She didn't have the right to disrespect you, and it's not an opinion with her, Professor—it's an agenda."

"What do you mean?"

"There's her way to look at things or there's her way to look at things."

"Hmm."

I have an earache and Sierra sits with me beside the open oven putting warm dry wash cloths on my ear. My head is on her lap. Finn slouches in the doorway.

"I told you this would happen." Sierra changes the wash-cloth, and a soothing warmth penetrates my ear. "Chairman Mao was right about motherly affection—it only diverts you from the ideals of the revolution. You needed to be at that rally." He swears and kicks the doorframe. "I told you to abort her early on."

Sierra puts her hand over my ear to block the noise of Finn's voice.

"I know about agendas, Mr. Kimball."

We walk beside each other in a long silence.

"Is there something else?"

"There is." He hesitates, "Do you mind if I ask a favor?"

"I may, depending on what it is."

"Would you mind calling me, Donavan?"

"Your first name?"

"Yes. Mr. Kimball makes me sound old, and I know we're about the same age."

"Hmm."

"I'll understand if you can't because of protocol or something, but…"

"There's no protocol. I call students by both first and last names."

"Terrific!"

"It's not a problem. But I may call you either Donavan or Mr. Kimball depending on the place and circumstance."

"Of course."

"And you won't be allowed to call me by my first name."

"No, of course not, Professor."

We stop in front of the building that houses my office. "Now, I have a question for you, Mr. Kimball…ah Donavan."

"Okay."

"Why is Dr. Lee your counselor? You're a math and physics major."

"He's a friend of my family. My dad deals with Asian antiquities."

"Ah."

"Over the years they've become friends." He waves to a group of peers. "Hey guys!" They wave back. "I guess he figured Dr. Lee could keep me in line."

"The Chinese Dragon."

Donavan laughs and I flinch. "Oh, sorry. Did that bother you?"

"Sudden noises are unsettling."

"I'll take note."

"Never mind, Donavan. People have to live their lives. I

can't expect the world to be a quiet oasis." I glance over and find Mr. Kimball staring at me. "Something wrong?"

"Ah…no. No, nothing wrong. It's just that…" He sticks his hands in the pockets of his hoodie. "I find you fascinating, Professor."

"Excuse me?"

"Oh! I don't mean it that way. I just meant that you're a fascinating person. So accomplished at your age." He looks at his friends. "So…anyway…"

I don't know how to answer him.

"I guess I'm off, then."

"You're not sure?"

"Huh?"

"Not sure that you're going?"

"Oh! Yes, I'm sure." He walks away, still talking. "I'll see you next class, Professor. I'm glad the President didn't call you in." He waves and joins his friends.

I turn and go into the building.

Actually, the President did call me in. I think about the uncomfortable meeting. He assured me that my position was not in jeopardy but warned that I was not to allow certain ideologies to be favored in the classroom. Which meant certain ideologies were not favored at all and should be blocked.

I climb the stairs to my office.

My feet stamp and I feel a scream snaking up my spine. Sierra tries to calm me, but not even Ganesha will do. I am six and Finn is threatening to throw my books in the trash.

"I'm sick of her quoting stuff to me!" Finn yells, "She's a kid!"

"I know. I'm sorry. I'll talk to her."

"Are you kidding? There's no talking to her."

Sierra pulls me behind her. "Just give her the books back and she'll stop."

"I swear, Sierra, you'd better get her under control."

"I will. I promise."

Finn throws the books on the floor, and I stop stamping. I pick up Ganesha, gather my property, and walk to my bedroom.

My books. I find sanctuary in my office and my books. I look at the picture of Baba and Dadi in traditional dress, images from the Hubble and James Web space telescopes, and the microscopic photo of a snowflake—a universe by design.

I sit in my chair and pull my quote diary from the drawer. I flip it open and read. "As long as you are proud you cannot know God. A proud man is always looking down on things and people: and, of course, as long as you are looking down, you cannot see something that is above you."

My phone chortles. "Hello?"

It is my uncle Aakesh. His voice is rushed and he asks me where I am. It makes me anxious, but I take a breath and answer him calmly. "In my office reading C.S. Lewis."

He tells me that Baba will pick me up in front of my building in ten minutes. He is going to the hospital with

Elly. Baby Yash is coming early, and Elly wants the family there for support. I want to ask a question, but he hangs up.

I fumble my phone into my pocket and gather my belongings. I am thinking about human gestation. No one needs to panic. The baby will be small but fully formed.

Elly has no make-up on, but there is a light in her face. Baby Yash in her arms. I turn to look at Aakesh who's face looks…I mentally search for the expression from my chart…astonished?

The baby's eyes are open. He was born only three hours ago and he's already showing an interest in the world. I look at the ceiling where he's looking. Are there glow stars and planets?

"Would you like to hold him?"

"Me?"

She maneuvers him towards me and I step back. "Me?" I say again.

Baba is at my shoulder. "You'll be fine."

My fists relax as I take him.

"Support his head," Aakesh demands.

Now he looks…worried.

I mimic Elly as I hold Yash Jha. Baba pats my shoulder. Thirty seconds and I give him back.

Elly beams at me. "Well done," she whispers.

I smile briefly and step back so Baba can have his turn. I am sure my birth scene was nothing like this.

Nine

I HOLD UP A GLOBE of the earth. It was given to me by Baba on my thirteenth birthday—on a stand—set at the correct angle, and it spins. I am spinning it now as my twenty-three students look on.

"At the equator the earth spins at one thousand miles per hour, and a day for us is twenty-four hours."

I point to Washington State and slowly spin the sphere. "Because it takes twenty-four hours to complete one rotation." I pick up Saturn affixed to a metal pole. "Saturn, which is much larger than Earth, spins faster—twenty-two thousand miles per hour. It takes ten and a half hours for one rotation, which means your time in this class would last about nineteen minutes."

The students chuckle. "I see that some of you wish this class was taking place on Saturn."

I catch a wink from Mr. Kimball which makes me mentally stumble. "So…so, we are talking about spheres and how the universe loves them: planets, atoms, water droplets, soap bubbles."

I bring up a picture of soap bubbles on the power point. "Your third assignment for next class…"

The students groan.

"…is a half-page paper on why soap bubbles are spherical."

I set down Saturn and give the earth a spin.

Sierra wakes up beside me on my bed.

"What are you doing?" Her words sound like they've come through syrup.

I continue pointing at my neon cosmos on the ceiling, my arm making slow circles. I'm seven and something is wrong. "They don't have points, you know."

"What don't?" Sierra asks groggily.

"Stars. Actually, they're big blobs of gas made spherical by gravity.

"But they're pretty with points. I like how they twinkle."

"Hmm."

She turns on her side to look at me. "What does Ganesha think."

I find Ganesha and set him on my chest. "He thinks they're pretty with points."

"See? And he's a god so he should know." She briefly lays her fingertips on the side of my face. "Why are you awake?"

"Thinking." I look up and find Saturn. "Sierra?"

"Yes."

"I will always be different, right?"

"What do you mean, Paige?"

"I will never be like Melanie."

"Melanie? The neighbor kid?" Ganesha nods for me. Sierra pauses. "No. You won't."

"Oh."

Sierra makes a growling noise in her throat. "Melanie's sub-normal. She sucks her thumb and at eight she still can't read. You want to be like her?"

"No."

"Well, I would hope not." Sierra sits up with her back against the wall. I mimic her. "Listen Paige, you're always going to be different. Your mind is like 'Lucy in the Sky with Diamonds.'" I like the image. "You might cure cancer or travel to Saturn." She rests her hand lightly on mine, and for once, Ganesha and I snuggle closer. "Most people are average…"

"Average—of the usual or ordinary standard."

"Exactly. And you will never be that." She gets up.

"Where are you going?"

"Bathroom. Then back to Finn."

"But I need you here."

"You'll be fine. Have Ganesha sing you a lullaby."

"But he…" She's gone. "He only knows Bollywood," I whisper so I don't offend him.

The bell rings, attended shortly by the usual scuffle and mummer of voices. A few of the students approach me with questions about the three assignments. I glance up to see Mr. Kimball laughing with a fellow student as they load their back packs.

Carissa. She is a girl with long blond hair that looks like it's been ironed. She is wearing a baby doll dress, bright patterned knee socks, and clunky shoes. I pull at the hem of my drab sweater wishing for once my brown hair wasn't braided like a rope down my back.

"Mr. Kimball?" His head turns at my voice.

"Yes, Professor?"

"I need to speak with you about your lab project."

"Sure. Okay." He says some last words to Carissa, who nods and smiles.

I don't like her teeth—too straight.

I answer the final student's question as Mr. Kimball makes his way to me. Just as he arrives at the well of the lecture hall, Dr. Lee enters from the teacher's door, nearly colliding with him. They share an awkward moment, then laugh and shake hands.

They move towards me.

Click click click.

I notice Donovan looking at my pen; I throw it in my satchel. "Dr. Lee? Why are you here?"

"Just came to say hello. How'd the class go?"

"I…well, I…"

"Much better without Miss Radical here," Mr. Kimball offers.

"Please, don't put words in my mouth, Mr. Kimball."

He looks down. "Sorry, Professor."

Dr. Lee grins. "Has Miss Everett dropped your class?"

"No. She is on vacation with her family."

Donavan growls. "Worse the luck she'll be back by next class."

"Now, Mr. Kimball…"

"Sorry, Professor," he says with wide eyes. A crooked grin crosses his lips.

He confuses me. Is he sorry or isn't he sorry?

Dr. Lee suppresses a smile. "No, *I'm* sorry. Did I interrupt something?"

"Just a consult about a lab project," I say in a rush.

"Go on then. I'll wait."

My thoughts tumble as Mr. Kimball fixes his eyes on me. He looks at the floor and I take a deep breath. "Your project relies heavily on math, Donavan."

He nods. "It does."

"Will you need tutoring?"

He glances up. "From you?"

Dr. Lee smiles.

"Ah, no. Not from me, but perhaps from my grandfather. He was a math professor here and I thought if you were perplexed on an equation…"

Donavan gives me a puzzled look and I stop talking. I look again and there's that crooked grin at the corner of his mouth. "Help from your grandfather?"

"Only if you…"

"Are you kidding? I would love it!" He seems to suppress his excitement. "It would be an honor. I've read some of his papers, and…"

Dr. Lee claps him on the shoulder. "I think that's a yes, Professor Jha."

"Good. I'll have him contact you. He may need you to come to his house if it's a longer consult. Would that be a problem?"

Donovan beams. "Not at all. Not. At. All. Thank you, Professor. Thank you."

"You're welcome."

He throws his backpack strap over his shoulder. "Wow." He turns and sprints up the stairs.

Dr. Lee raises his eyebrows, "You've just made someone's day."

"I'm glad I can help."

"Hope Avi feels the same."

"You know that Baba will give me anything I want." I finish putting away my belongings.

"This is true," Dr. Lee gives me a wink.

I point at his eye. "I don't understand this gesture."

He picks up my computer bag. "Winking?"

"Yes, winking. What does it mean? I understand? I think you're right? There's a secret between us?"

"Any of the above."

I grumble and start walking. "Confusing."

"I would imagine." Dr. Lee chuckles and follows. "You haven't been around many people until now."

"I did attend college, you remember."

"And how many of your peers interacted with you in college?"

"I didn't have peers."

"Exactly."

"And what was that look, Mr. Kimball gave me? The look before saying thank you. It's not in my picture collection of expressions."

Dr. Lee holds the door open for me and waits while I count. "That's because it was a combination of looks—wonder, delight, gratitude, warmth."

"Warmth?" I ask quizzically.

"If I read it correctly."

"I don't know what that means."

"All for the better. At least I need not raise a voice of warning yet."

I stop and look him in the face. "What in the world are you going on about?"

He winks.

"Stop that!"

A low chuckle escapes his throat. "Let's talk about this month's faculty get together."

"Not going."

"Paige."

"No. Not going. The luncheon was a disaster—binary stars in which I was the dying red giant."

"It wasn't that bad."

"It wasn't? You were standing right by me with the group of tenured professors."

"You seemed only slightly nervous."

"Slightly? I was nonstop talking for ten minutes about

the electromagnetic spectrum, infra-red light and ultraviolet light."

Dr. Lee grins. "It was interesting."

"It was not. One by one they just started drifting away to other groups or the buffet table."

"A few stayed for your expose on Roger Penrose and Penrose tiling."

An unexpected growl rumbles in my throat. I shake my head. "No. Not going." I walk to the main entrance door, open it, count to four, and step out. The courtyard is misted in fog.

Dr. Lee follows. "But it's the Harvest Dinner, Paige. You deserve to go. You've worked hard."

"No. They don't like me."

"Why do you think that?"

"I've lived with this long enough to know a few things, Professor, and I know I make them uncomfortable."

"Paige Jha!" he snaps.

"No. I don't fit. I'm too young—too odd."

"So, there were no Lotus Flowers at the luncheon?"

I quickly evaluate. "Two. You and Professor Whitmore from the English department. We talked about C.S. Lewis, and she didn't seem bored."

"Well, that's a start! Come to the dinner and I'll make sure you're seated between me and Professor Whitmore."

I hesitate. "No." I take my computer bag from him and walk away.

He stops walking because he has a class, but he calls after

me. "You hesitated! That means a part of you wants to go!"

"Not one molecule of me wants to go!"

"There will be crab! You love crab!"

"Go teach your class, parrot monster!" I take cover in the fog.

Ten

N ot this nightmare.
I try to wake myself before it overwhelms me.
Please. Please. Please. Not this.

My ice cream melts. I watch the stranger sleeping on the sand. I lay my yellow book on his outstretched hand and wait.

"Please Paige, don't wake him," Sierra says. She holds her hands in front of her like she's saying a prayer. "Eat your ice cream."

I hold it out.

"Don't you want it?"

"No. No, thank you. It's too soft."

"That's because you didn't eat it right away." Sierra holds out her hand and wiggles her fingers. "Give it here. I'll eat it."

Finn grumbles. "I told you not to buy it for her." His eyes open. "She was never gonna eat it with all this sand."

Sierra doesn't answer, her tongue too busy managing the dripping ice cream.

"Well, that's sexy." Finn sits up, the yellow book sliding

into the sand unnoticed. He gets out a joint and searches for his lighter.

Sierra stops eating and stares at him.

"What? We're practically alone. Besides the Washington legislators are gonna cave any day."

"But, not yet. Do you want to go to jail?"

"Nobody's going to jail."

"And what about Paige?"

"No ten-year-old is going to jail." He laughs at his joke.

She tosses the cone away. "Not funny, and it's not what I meant."

"I know." He lights up and I smell singed oregano on a hot electric burner. He takes a deep drag on the joint and speaks on half a breath like an asthmatic. "Come on. We came to the beach to relax." He crawls over to her. "Here, let me lick the ice cream off your face."

"Stop it, Finn!" she hisses. Then a grin at the side of her mouth. Her eyes fix on his as he pushes her back. "But, Paige—" he covers her mouth with his hand.

A bird screeches overhead and Finn smiles. "Hey, P. What's that bird?"

I look where he's pointing. "American kestrel."

"So, tell us what you know about that little fellow." He yanks my quilt from under me and pulls it over them.

I stand, brushing the sand off my pants. "Species: F. sparverius, genius: Falco. The American kestrel is usually found in close proximity to open fields, either perched on a snag or telephone wire or hovering in search of prey."

There are moans from under the quilt.

"The typical falcon-shaped wings are slim and pointed;

the tail long and square-tipped." Sierra whimpers and my stomach clinches.

I move towards the ocean. "Sexes are of similar size. Adult male plumage is easily told from adult females and juveniles of both sexes."

The kestrel screeches overhead. I pick up a smooth beach stone and throw it skyward. I know it will never reach him, but I throw another and another and another.

I scream and beat my hand against my mattress.

Baba rushes in. He sits me up and wraps his arms around me from behind. He smells like spice and onion. He squeezes me tight and I stop screaming. He loosens his grip and my breathing slows.

"Bad dream?" he asks.

I nod slowly.

"You haven't had one of those in a while."

I turn to him and nod assurance that I'm okay. I breathe deeply and smell spices. "Are you cooking, Baba?"

He smiles. "Aloo Paratha."

Unexpected tears run down my cheeks.

Baba takes the dishcloth from his shoulder and wipes them away as if from a china plate. "So, splash some water on your face and come to breakfast in your pajamas. You can get ready for work after."

I am twelve and eating Aloo Paratha for the first time at Baba's breakfast table. I stare out at the Sound through the large picture window. I lay down my fork and go to look at the water. There is a ship moving through the Sound towards the open ocean.

"Where is it going?"

Baba stops washing dishes. "Are you speaking in sentences now?"

"Yes."

He comes to stand beside me. "Maybe Alaska."

"Alaska. Northern most state of the United States. Established in 1959. The state capitol is Juneau."

"Interesting." Baba and I stand quietly watching the ship on its way to Alaska. Then Baba asks me a question. "What color is the water?"

I stand mute. I don't know how to answer this.

Baba leaves my side and goes to the garage, returning with a fan deck of paint colors. He hands it to me. "See if you can find it in here."

I spend an hour comparing colors. I finally decide and announce the name to Baba. "Celestial."

I walk to my class with the patter of rain on my umbrella. There is an ache in the back of my head from a troubled night's sleep and I stretch my neck to ease some of the stiffness. It's difficult to focus but I need to review today's lesson from *Tao Te Ching—The Way*. How does one teach a thing unteachable? I'm again with Sir Isaac, wandering as a child on the vast shores of knowledge. One drop in the immense ocean of thought.

"The philosophy of Tao would say 'In his every movement a man of great virtue follows The Way and The Way only. As a thing The Way is shadowy, indistinct…'"

"What are you mumbling, Professor?"

I am yanked from my thoughts. "Oh! Mr. Kimball! Donavan."

"Sorry. Didn't mean to sneak up on you. I need to remember to give you a heads up."

"Why are you here? You don't have my next class."

"This is true, but I wanted to talk with you."

"About?"

"About your grandfather. He called me."

I start to walk. "He said he would."

Mr. Kimball's umbrella follows along. "He set our first meeting—Saturday night at his house. Well…your house too, right?"

"Hmm."

"Will you be there?"

"Yes. Where else would I be?"

"Sorry, Professor. Am I interrupting you?"

"You are. I was going over my upcoming lesson."

"Oh! Oh, sorry. I'll leave you to it, Professor." He goes back the way we came. "We can talk later."

"Thank you, Donavan." He heads off and I continue my evaluation of The Way.

An angry snarl of voices erupts on the opposite side of the courtyard. I turn to my left and watch as a man steps from a van and is immediately surrounded by police. The protestors move in, shouting and shaking their signs. The crowd advances and follows the man across the courtyard. I want to move; to run, but the sound presses against my body, keeping me in place. So much noise. So much movement. A frozen water bottle slams into my umbrella, ripping it from my hand. I attempt to steady myself as a scream strangles in my throat. I try to stamp like Ganesha, when someone yells into my face, "A woman's body—a woman's choice!"

I forget how to stamp. Several women spit at the man in the center of their fury. They throw things. They scream and shove at the police. I call out as bodies bump against me and hands hit my face.

Someone wraps their arms tightly around me and pulls me back.

"It's all right, Professor. It's all right. I have you."

The four arms of Shiva protecting. Tighter. Hold me tighter.

His arms tighten; it's as though my thoughts escaped my brain—sound waves traveling through space. The arms pull me back and the angry voices move away. Suddenly, I hear only the patter of rain. It soaks my hair, my face, and drips down my back. I shiver.

The grip loosens slightly, and I breathe.

"Let's get you inside," a warm whisper against my ear.

I turn my body in his arms. *Mr. Kimball?*

His face is close to mine. I whisper, "How did you know to hold me like that?"

He slowly releases me. "I read that it helps." He picks up his umbrella.

I unclench my fists and realize my fingers have gone stiff with cold. "I need to get to my class."

"Let's get you to your office. You're drenched, and besides, I'm pretty sure classes will be canceled for the next several hours."

"Canceled. To decide that an organized event will not happen…"

"Yeah. Not safe with that gang stomping around protesting free speech." He puts his hand on my back, and I shrug away.

"Sorry, Professor." We start walking. "And, sad to say, it looks like Miss Everett is back from vacation."

I stop. "What?"

"Kennedy's back. She was the one who screamed in your face."

"Oh." I feel the ache of cold in my body.

"That girl is a misery," said Donavan.

"Mr. Kimball," I scold.

"Sorry, but she is. I know I'm not supposed to judge, but she gets under my skin."

I'm shivering.

"Hey, let's get going before you freeze to death."

"A core body temperature would need to be below 95 degrees for hypothermia to set in."

His blank expression almost makes me smile.

"Well, let's not take any chances."

We walk together under his umbrella. We pass mine laying useless on the grass—the spokes bent like a bird's broken wing.

Eleven

"Last class we were to discuss the *Tao Te Ching* or *The Way*, but classes were canceled because a few students were protesting."

"Actually, there were more than a few of us," a student argues—an edge to her voice.

"I take it you participated, Miss Fennimore."

"I did. First Amendment. Freedom of speech," she gloats.

"I applaud freedom of speech, but I didn't witness free speech or a peaceable assembly. Your protest seemed more like intimidation."

"Excuse me?"

"You were stomping around campus attempting to intimidate an invited guest from speaking."

"Stomping around?" Her voice has a furious edge.

The class stills as though holding its breath.

Another student wades in. "But, Professor Jha, you said your teaching philosophy is to test and measure everything."

"That's right, Mr. Flansberg."

"And that everyone has a right to an opinion."

I nod in agreement.

"Didn't the protestors have a right to their opinion?"

"Of course. But they weren't interested in participating in a discussion of opinions, they were only interested in stopping the other person from having or voicing an opinion."

"Because his opinion was crap," Miss Fennimore snaps.

A few of the class members clap, while others murmur.

"There seems to be a difference of opinion," I point out.

"So, we're just supposed to let him spew his garbage?"

"Many of us didn't see it as garbage," offers Miss Aston.

"That's because you're an idiot."

"Miss Fennimore!"

"Oh, sorry, Professor. Just stating my opinion."

I attempt a response, but I can feel my heart thumping against my ribs and my thoughts beginning to fray.

"Never mind, Professor," Miss Aston intervenes. "Sticks and stones. I'm far more interested in your thoughts on The Way."

I look directly at Lydia Aston's smiling face and breathe. "Thank you, Miss Aston."

My hands shake as I turn to my computer and bring up a picture of a path leading into a forest. "Let's look at what Lao Tzu says about this path, which isn't a path. An essence unknowable except to the person who is already in The Way. A thing unteachable."

"Wow. This is going to be exciting," Miss Fennimore mutters—her annoyance thick.

I hear her but pretend I don't.

The heavy fog from the ocean is biting as I move across campus to Dr. Lee's office. I don't want to talk with him today. I don't want to share or listen. Leopard in a cage—jumpy and unsettled. I tried to teach about "The Way," but Miss Fennimore's defiant face kept presenting itself. "The Way" became a shadow of a shadow.

I walk past two girls hunched in their coats, giggling and speaking gibberish. As I pass them, I smell oregano burning on a hot burner. I stop and turn back. The girl with white spiky hair brings the joint to her lips. I snatch it out of her hand and throw it down.

"Hey!"

"That will kill you."

"You're nuts!" She picks the joint off the ground.

Her friend shoves my shoulder. "Get away from us, weirdo!"

"That will kill you!"

They walk quickly away, casting angry glances back at me.

Ganesha and I watch unnoticed as Sierra kneels on the front room floor and shoves the couch to the side. She pulls up a square section of the wood laminate, the slats lifting together hinged at the back.

I ask Ganesha if he knows about this secret place, but he is quiet.

Sierra gets out a shoebox like Finn's money collecting

box. She throws off the lid and gets out the orange plastic tube. Her hands shake when she opens the white cap.

Ganesha tells me to run back to our room—quietly—no stamping. We crawl under the bed, and I lay my head on Ganesha's tummy. His breathing sounds like wind in a bamboo forest.

The cold nips at the flesh of my hands and I flex my fingers to make the blood flow. My feet are fixed in place as I watch the retreating students. I turn and see Miss Everett walking across campus. She stares at me—an odd twist to her lips. I am the Leopard.

Twelve

I MAKE NAAN FLATBREAD and watch Baba and Donavan at the dining room table. They are discussing the mapping of space. Well, Donavan is mostly listening and taking notes.

"Don't give him all the answers, Baba. Make him work."

"You there on the sidelines, you be quiet," Baba barks at me with a grin. "We are accomplishing marvelous things here. Mind your cooking and check the lobster bisque."

Donavan smiles over at me, then turns back to his notes. "This really is great stuff."

I stir the soup. "Hence the sage knows himself but does not display himself, loves himself but does not exalt himself."

The men laugh.

Baba wags his finger at me "Ah, you must be careful of that one, Donavan. She has an answer for everything."

"Smart *and* a good cook," says Donavan still smiling.

"Her?" Baba sputters. "Her cook? No-no-no. A black hole would have to be at the bottom of the pot for her to pay attention. No. I am the cook here."

I shake my head. "Hence the cook knows himself but does not exalt…"

"Quiet, Shurpanakha!"

"Who's that?" Donavan asks.

"A wicked ugly demoness who had her nose cut off for poking it into other people's business."

I replace the lid on the soup pot. "Besides, if there was a black hole at the bottom of this pot we would not exist."

Donavan laughs, then stops when he sees my face. "Oh, you were serious."

Baba shakes his head. "Jokes come rarely with her. I'm trying to teach her how to be funny."

"Well, *that* was funny. Nerd funny, but still funny." He smiles at me directly, which makes me uneasy.

I tap my finger on the counter. "You two need to finish. The family will be here soon for dinner."

"Would you like to join us, Mr. Kimball?" asks Baba.

I stretch a ball of dough into a flat disc. "I don't think that would be appropriate, Baba."

Donavan puts papers in his backpack. "No really, it's fine. She's right. I'm only here for the tutoring."

Baba stretches his back. "Nonsense. You need nourishment after your hard work."

"Hard work?"

"Hush, Shurpanakha before someone comes after *your* nose," Baba instructs. "Pay attention to your bread." He places a hand on Donavan's shoulder. "I insist, Mr. Kimball. I love to cook for other people and that one eats like a bird, my Little Twig."

"If you're sure it's no trouble."

"Of course not!"

I glare at the two of them and slap the disc of dough onto the grill pan. There is a knock at the door. "The baby's here!"

"Just the baby?" Baba questions. "Very independent of him."

The door opens and Aakesh calls out. "The troops have arrived!"

Donavan stands and backs towards the picture window. *I hope he's nervous to meet new people.*

"Are you sure it's okay for me to stay?"

I say no and Baba says yes at the same time. I flip the flatbread.

Aakesh and Elly enter the dining room with bags, blankets, a car seat, and baby Yash.

"Namaste," Elly says.

"Welcome family!" Baba greets as he takes the baby. "Come meet Donavan Kimball. He's one of Professor Jha's students."

"Really?" Aakesh glances over at me with a look I don't recognize. Eyes wider—crooked smile. It *seems* like surprise but not surprise.

"He's tall," Askesh says brightly. "What are you, six foot something?"

"Six, two."

Baba intervenes. "Donavan, this is my son Aakesh, his wife Elly, and my grandson Yash."

He brings Yash to me to say hello as Aakesh and Elly put down their baggage and exchange greetings and handshakes.

"Donavan's joining us for dinner," Baba announces.

"Wonderful!" says Elly. "You're one of Paige's students?"

"I'm in her physics class."

"She's amazing, isn't she?"

"She is."

I tap my tongs on the counter.

Books from the library surround me as I sit on my bedroom floor reading *The Voyage of the Dawn Treader*. Ganesha sits on a stack of science books and trumpets that he's
hungry and ready for lunch. He trumpets again and I hurry
to shut the door before Sierra and Finn hear him. I watch
and listen at the small opening.

"No nine-year-old needs to go to a special school."

"Paige does."

"Yeah? So? Where's the money coming from?"

"I'll ask my parents."

"Huh! They won't even help us pay rent. You think
they're gonna spring for a fancy school?"

"I think they will."

"Forget it. I don't want you talking to them. You hear me?"

"But..."

"No. Just send her to public school."

"She doesn't fit there, Finn."

"Tough. She's nothing special, so just forget about some
expensive snobby school."

I shut the door and turn to see that Ganesha has fallen
off his stack of books. I guess he fainted from hunger.

I flip the crusty piece of naan bread and continue tapping. "He's only here because Baba is helping him with some math equations. I didn't invite him for dinner."

"Well, thank you for clearing that up," Aakesh says with a grin. "Don't mind her, Mr. Kimball, she always says weird stuff."

"I do not."

"Let's eat!" Baba calls out. "Mr. Kimball, guests first. Grab a bowl and ladle your own soup. We're informal here."

I take a step away when Donavan comes to get his soup.

He lowers his voice. "Sorry, I didn't mean to cause a fuss."

"Hmm." I continue tapping. "Don't let your soup get cold."

He moves away; now I can breathe.

Elly comes with her bowl. "Paige, you can stop tapping," she whispers.

I do. I put the last piece of flatbread in the basket.

Elly holds out her hands. "I'll take that to the table."

I give it to her and she smiles.

"I think Mr. Kimball is nice."

"Nice: pleasant, agreeable, satisfactory."

"All of the above," Elly says, still smiling.

"Hmm."

Baba puts the sleeping Yash in his car seat and goes to get his soup. I move to the round table and find that Elly and Aakesh have seated themselves so that there are empty chairs only on either side of Donavan.

I sit.

Baba sets his soup down and pulls out his chair. "Elly, would you say blessing on the food?"

"Of course."

Donavan's eyes open wide. I know that look. He is surprised. "What did you think, Mr. Kimball? That we were, pagans?"

Elly and Aakesh snort with laughter.

I sit on the deck wrapped in one of Dadi's blankets. I hear the patio door scrape open.

"I'm on my way," Donavan's voice drifts out to me.

"Hmm." I hear the door scrape again, but then footsteps cross the deck. Mr. Kimball sits in the deck chair adjacent to mine."

"I didn't mean to be a bother, Professor."

"Hmm."

"Your grandfather is amazing and so kind; I didn't want to offend him."

"I understand, Mr. Kimball."

We sit in quiet as we look out over the darkness of the Sound.

Mr. Kimball clears his throat. "And, I have to admit that being here with you at a place other than school is nice."

"But inappropriate."

"Inappropriate? Really?"

I glance at him. "Of course, Mr. Kimball. We have a student teacher relationship. The rules set forth by the university are strict concerning intercourse."

Obviously startled, Mr. Kimball sits straighter. "Intercourse? Oh no. Excuse me, Professor, but…"

"Intercourse: communication or dealings between individuals or groups."

"Oh. Oh, I see." His face flushes and he slumps back into his chair. "Right." He puts his hand on his chest. "I respect the student teacher relationship—one hundred percent. But…I thought we might be friends."

"Friends? What does that mean?"

He gives me a half grin. "You know, people who hang out together, share stories, ask questions, give each other advice."

"Hmm."

"Don't you have friends?"

"I have Baba and Elly and Aakesh."

"Family is great, but it's not the kind of friendship I'm talking about."

"I have Dr. Lee."

"He's your mentor and sort of like family. Doesn't count."

"Why are you being so irritating?"

"I don't mean to be, Paige. I just feel you need a friend."

"You used my first name."

"I did. And I don't think the garden snails will report us to President Nowell."

"I don't know how to respond to you."

"Don't your Asian scholars have anything to say about friendship?"

"Confucius teaches us that there are three friends that do good and three friends that do harm."

"This sounds hopeful. Tell me about that."

"The three friends that do good are a straight friend, a sincere friend, and a friend who has heard much. The three friends that do harm are a smooth friend, a fawning friend, and a friend with a glib tongue."

"Smart guy, that Confucius."

"Hmm." I glance at him, and he smiles.

"I'd like to be your friend, Paige." He looks directly at me and leans forward. "Just a good friend. Is that possible?"

I'm looking at his mouth as he comes closer. I cover his lips with my hand, and he chuckles. From a distance comes the screech of a gull. I pull my hand away and bring the blanket up over my shoulders. "I will have to ask Baba."

Donavan sits straight up. "You're going to talk to your grandfather about this?'

"Of course."

The patio door opens, and Donavan jumps to his feet. Baba sticks his head out. "Aakesh and Elly are leaving."

I stand. "With the baby?"

Baba snorts. "Of course, with the baby, you goof. You think he can take a taxi?"

"I'm leaving too," Donavan announces in a rush. "I'll see you in class on Monday, Professor Jha." He heads for the house before I have a chance to answer.

Thirteen

I BRING UP AN IMAGE on the power point and chuckles percolate among the students.

"Today we're going to talk about *Harry Potter and the Deathly Hallows*, mandalas, the great blunder of Albert Einstein, and the two pillars of physics."

I hear the click of computer keys.

"Let's begin by taking a close look at this image of Mr. Lovegood's necklace—a circle and line within a triangle. The invisibility cloak…"

"Oh! We have a Harry Potter nerd for a professor," someone calls out good naturedly.

I turn and point at the usually quiet student with wire framed glasses and ears that stick out a bit from his head. "I'll take that as a compliment, Mr. Cameron."

He laughs as I turn my attention back to the image. "The triangle represents the Cloak of Invisibility; the line, the Elder Wand; the circle the Resurrection Stone. The line and the circle are circumscribed inside the triangle. It's a cosmological symbol."

I bring up an image of an equilateral triangle inside a circle. "Now, here is a triangle circumscribed within a circle. Notice how each point of the triangle touches on the line of the circle but does not penetrate."

"Professor?"

I stiffen at the sound of the voice.

"Yes, Miss Everett?" I look out to the students and find her face. The plug in her bottom lip seems to be infected. I start to comment on it, then remember how angry it made her when I referenced her lip.

My pen.

Click click click

"Is there a point to all this?"

I take a breath. "There is, Kennedy. In cosmology there is a theory dealing with a circumscribed universe."

I bring up another image of a square inside a circle. "Remember at the beginning of the term when I had you each color a mandala?"

I bring up an image of an intricately painted Tibetan mandala of a square inside a circle. "Legend has it that the genesis of the mandala began with Siddhartha Gautama around 500 B.C with his enlightenment and journey to become Buddha."

"Ah…this is physics 105, Professor," Miss Everett sneers. "Did you forget what class you were in?"

Mr. Kimball slams his book shut. "Hey, Kennedy! The rest of us are interested. So, stop interrupting?"

"How sweet. The boyfriend coming to her defense."

A few whistles and cat calls swirl around the room.

I raise my voice. "Mandalas are symbols of a person's journey to find truth, enlightenment, and an ever-deepening insight into self and into the universe."

Kennedy snorts. "So weird."

I lay my pen down. "Miss Everett?"

She frowns at me.

"Did Einstein ever make a mistake?"

She scowls. "What do you mean?"

"In all his brilliant calculations, did Einstein ever make a mistake?"

She shifts in her seat. "I haven't studied all his calculations."

"An appropriate answer."

A hand flies into the air.

"Yes, Mr. Cameron."

"I can answer that, Professor."

"Miss Everett, do you mind if Mr. Cameron answers the question?"

She shrugs one shoulder. "Whatever."

Mr. Cameron jumps in. "He did make a mistake. In fact, he called it his biggest blunder. It was when he added the idea of a cosmological constant to the theory of an expanding universe."

"Thank you, Mr. Cameron." I bring up the famous image of Einstein sticking out his tongue. The students laugh.

"So, mistakes were made; a scientific theory called into question. As a scientist you must always be willing to test a theory." I move to an image from the Hubble telescope of thousands of galaxies spinning in space. "Is the universe a circumscribed sphere? Is it negative curvature resembling a saddle, or is it flat?"

I write on the board.

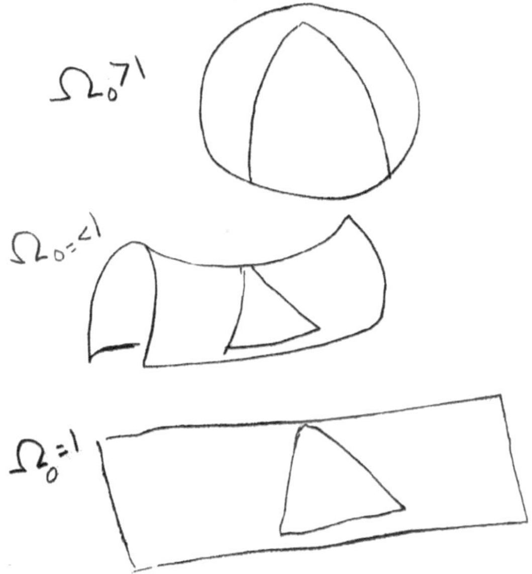

I turn around and find blank stares.

"Go back to the Resurrection Stone," a student calls out and the class laughs.

But I don't laugh. My mind has wandered off to mandalas, death, and the circumscribed universe.

Sierra takes off her long black skirt, shoving it into the back of the dresser drawer. She puts on Levis.

"Not one word to Finn about where we've been."

I crawl up onto her bed. "Why not?"

"You heard him. He told me not to go."

"It was Dadi's funeral. Why does he have a say?"

"You're eleven-years-old, Paige. You understand what goes on and how he is." Her head droops down and she rubs her hands over her face. She moans as though her heart is being squeezed. "I don't know a way out." Tears strangle in her throat.

I look at the front door. "You could go there."

Her head swivels slowly so she's looking at the door. "Not likely."

My stomach growls. "There was food at Baba's house. Why didn't we stay? I'm hungry."

Sierra rummages in her big bag and gets out an aluminum foil wrapped package. "Here, I snatched some sandwiches before leaving." Ganesha and I reach for them. "Take them to your room." Her voice sounds shaky like she's about to cry again. "And not one word about where we went. Got it?"

I nod. "But Ganesha might say something."

"I swear, Paige, if he does, I'm grinding him in the garbage disposal!" She starts sobbing and Ganesha and I back away quickly. We reach the room and I shut the door. I don't cry, but it takes a long time to unwrap the sandwiches.

I focus on the faces of my students, then up to the power point picture of a thousand spinning galaxies. Baba warned me that I might be skipping chapters. I take a breath and put down the marker. I turn back to the class. "Sorry, was that too complex?"

"Light years ahead of us," says Mr. Isakson.

"You might want to go back to the Periodic Table," Mr. Kimball adds with a smile.

"Well, I won't go back that far, but let's go to a flawless Einstein and a brilliant Dr. Planck." I pass over several slides on my power point until I come to photos of Albert Einstein and Max Planck. "Mr. Kimball, can you tell us the two pillars of modern physics?"

He looks directly at me. "Relativity and quantum mechanics."

"Exactly right. Einstein gave us the theory of relativity and Max Planck and his team gave us quantum mechanics. These we will discuss, but first…" I bring a quote onto the screen. "Mr. Cameron, would you please read the statement by Mr. Planck?"

"Science cannot solve the ultimate mystery of nature. And that is because, in the last analysis, we ourselves are part of the mystery that we are trying to solve."

"That should incline us towards humility, shouldn't it, Mr. Cameron?"

"Yes, Professor."

I look up. Several heads nod and I hear a few voices saying "cool" or "awesome." Never-the-less, one student slouches in her chair, arms folded across her chest, glaring at me.

"Dr. Lee, could I ask you a favor?"

"Of course, Professor Jha."

"Would you put that statue in a drawer?"

He reaches immediately for the newest addition to his collection. "You're not fond of Kali?"

Goddess of time, creation, and destruction.

I study the blue goddess; her many arms holding weapons and a severed head—her red tongue dangling from her mouth. I stare at my shoes. "No, I am not fond of her. She is hideous."

I hear the desk drawer open and shut. I look up.

Dr. Lee chuckles. "Well, I did pay a hideous price for her."

"I would ask Mr. Kimball for your money back."

Now he laughs. "And Avi says you're not funny."

"I'm not funny, but sometimes I state facts and they're funny."

"Astute deduction." He leans forward. "But how do you know my broker?"

"I know his son, Donavan. He's in my physics class."

"Ah. Of course. That's right." He sits back in his chair and folds his arms across his chest. "I hope you two aren't talking about me behind my back."

"We are, but nothing harmful. I just asked him why you were his counselor, and he told me your connection to his father. He said his father wants you to scare him into being a stellar student."

"I'm doing my best, Professor Jha. And what do you think of him?"

"Sorry?"

"The *young* Mr. Kimball, is he a stellar student?"

"He is. I wish all my students were as diligent."

"And Miss Everett? Are you still having trouble with her?"

I press my palms together. "She's not bad academically, but…"

"But?"

"I just wonder why she dislikes me so fervently."

"A legitimate conundrum, Professor. Maybe it's because you're a hundred times smarter than she is, maybe because your ancestorial family is from India, or because the other students think you're awesome. Or maybe because you're too tall or too short, or you like yellow, and she likes green. Sometimes there's no figuring it out."

"Hmm."

"I once had a student transfer out of my class because he didn't like my accent. Said it bugged him."

"Absurd."

He shrugs. "Like I said, hard to figure."

"I think Miss Everett doesn't see me as a role model."

"Truly?"

My thoughts go back to the cold rainy day and her screaming at me during the protest. "Maybe because she's a dissident and I'm…I'm not."

"No, you're not." He winks at me.

I frown. "Now, what does *that* wink mean?"

"Encouragement." His face takes on a more serious look.

"Just be careful of her—steer clear of confrontation."

"Hmm."

"Now, before time's up, I want to know how you liked the Harvest Banquet."

I look at Dr. Lee's expectant face. "I liked the crab. The crab was good."

The tangy smell of salt water and baking sea food assaults my nose and I keep breathing deeply.

"Hey, stop that or you'll pass out!" Finn barks. I stop. "So, what do you want?"

"Food?"

"Yeah, food. You made a lot a money today, so we're getting street lunch."

I look at the menu board.

"Ya want me to help you, little girl?" A man in a white plastic apron asks.

"Okay, so here's the deal," Finn breaks in. "If she can read your menu board, you give her a free crab lunch."

"With fries," I add.

"With fries."

"The man chuckles. "What is she, five?"

"Just."

"Okay, it's a deal—steamed crab legs with fries." He glances around at other potential customers who are gathering. "This I gotta see."

Finn taps me on the head. "Go on then, Einstein."

"Fish and chips, fish stew, crab legs 2, 4, or 6, crab sandwich with slaw…"

"How's she doing that?" the apron man asks, as more people gather around.

"Fish sandwich with slaw, crab cakes, clams on the half shell. Draft beer $2 with any order."

I come to the end of the menu. The people clap and comment as the apron man pounds Finn on the shoulder.

"She's a freaking genius! Wow! That was something." He raises his voice. "In honor of this smart kid I'm going to do a genius discount for the next hour! Two bucks off your order or a free beer!"

The customers line up. The man turns to us with a lot of teeth showing. "Take a seat at that table and I'll bring your order out."

"Thanks," Finn says. "And I'll take a free beer."

"Sure thing! "Coming right up!"

We sit at the table with a plastic tablecloth in red and white squares. Finn lifts me onto the wooden stool. My feet can't touch the ground, so I kick them back and forth.

"Finn?"

"Huh?"

"Will I like crab?"

He shrugs. "I don't know. If you don't, I'll eat it for you."

"Okay."

"You can have the French fries."

"The crab was good."

Dr. Lee smiles. "The whole buffet was terrific! And the company?"

"Professor Whitmore was nice."

"Well, there you go! Crab and a nice conversation with Dr. Whitmore about C.S. Lewis."

"Actually, we talked about Tolkien."

"Ah, new subject matter as well! You *are* making progress, Professor."

"Am I?"

There's a knock on the office door.

"Ah." He winks. "My broker's son."

"Mr. Kimball?"

"We have a consult." Dr. Lee heads for the door.

I stand. "I'll be going, then."

"Next time, Paige, I'd like to go over your curriculum planning." He opens the door. "Come in, Mr. Kimball. Professor Jha and I were just talking about you!"

Heat flashes on my face and I look at the floor. I busy myself picking up my computer bag and satchel. Donavan's tennis shoes come into my field of vision.

"Nothing negative, I hope?"

I edge to the door. "No. Actually, we only spoke of you briefly and how Dr. Lee and your father are acquainted." I grasp the door handle. "No need to be concerned."

I open the door, count to four, and step into the hallway. "No need at all."

I snap the door shut and head for the cold of outside and the bus stop. I wonder what Baba is making for dinner as I try to control my breathing.

Fourteen

STIFF GREEN LEATHER looks expensive but it is not a comfortable material for a couch. It causes one to sit straight and fidget. Perhaps that's President Nowell's intention. Make the person sitting in his office as uncomfortable as possible.

The door opens, and the President is removing his coat as he comes rushing in, "Sorry. I'm late."

"Twenty-two minutes."

"Right. Twenty-two minutes. Sorry. My meeting with the board went over." He hangs his coat and straightens his tie as he moves to his desk. "Come sit over here, Professor Jha."

An upholstered green leather chair awaits me. "It's not comfortable."

"What? Oh yes, probably not." We both sit. "Did my secretary offer you anything?"

"Yes, but I wasn't thirsty."

"Ah…right." He opens a desk drawer and brings out a file.

"Does that have my name on it?"

"It does."

"Does every teacher have a file?"

"Of course."

"Even, Dr. Lee?"

"Don't be nervous, Professor Jha. We're just here to clear up a few reports."

"Reports?"

"First," he leans forward. "Just a general question. Do you like being a teacher?"

I look at my shoes. "Most of the time."

"Most of the time? Can you elaborate?"

"I don't like grading papers, and it bothers me when the students don't try. I do like offering new information and when we discuss topics."

I think back to discussions on the expansion of the universe, of dark matter and the Confucian teachings of man's nobility and responsibility.

"Professor Jha?"

I sit straighter and look at him. "Yes?"

"Are you with me?"

"I am. I'm here in your office." I tap my finger on the arm of the chair. "Yes, I like teaching. I like it very much."

"I see." He writes on a notepad. "And you get along with your students?"

"I don't know what that means."

"Do they like you?"

"I don't know. I think a few of them do not."

"Interesting." He opens the file and I see papers with sentences; some underlined in red—the color of stop or warning. He picks up one of the papers and peruses it. "Now, we have the prior report of you being unable to manage your classroom and allowing offending dogma to be preached."

"Offending: causing problems or displeasure. An illegal act or the breaking of a rule."

The president looks up from his papers. "I beg your pardon?"

"You never actually told me which of my students was offended. I can guess, but you never said who filed the complaint."

"That is in the past."

"But you gave me a warning which is still in effect."

"Yes. I remember. Just a caution, really."

Another paper.

"*Now* a student has reported that, in front of her peers, you belittled her First Amendment rights of freedom of speech and peaceable assembly."

"I only pointed out the difference between peaceable assembly and intimidating protest."

"It is a fine line to tread, Professor Jha. Perhaps it's out of your depths; something you can't navigate."

"Hmm."

He shuffles his papers and I look at my shoes again as he continues. "It's also reported by two people that they witnessed you striking a student on campus."

I look up quickly and find him staring at me. "No,

President, I did not. I would never hit a student."

"The report says you slapped the female student's hand."

"No, I didn't."

Spikey white hair and the smell of oregano on a hot burner.

"I just took something dangerous out of her hand."

"And your hand never made contact with hers?"

I can't answer that question.

"I…I don't know."

"I see." He pulls out another piece of paper. "Now, this report is especially troublesome, Professor." He shakes his head. "You are aware of the code of conduct for every teacher at this university."

"Yes, of course."

"Well, this report says you were seen on campus being hugged by a male student."

"What?" I try to breathe but there is no air in my lungs. The word comes out in a smothered whisper. I tap my chest trying to calm my thumping heart.

I need to talk to Baba.

There is a knock at the door and Dr. Lee pops his head in. "Dr. Nowell, may I have a word?"

"Not now, Jacob. I'm with a teacher."

Dr. Lee steps into the room and closes the door behind him. "Yes, that's why I'm here."

"You can't just barge in and interrupt a consult."

"And you know you can't interrogate this particular teacher without first notifying me."

"I'm not interrogating anyone!"

"Sorry. You can't *consult* with this particular teacher without first notifying me. It's in her contract."

"There were some reports that needed immediate attention." President Nowell's voice scrapes against my ears.

Dr. Lee nods. "Let me have a moment to assess them." He reaches for the folder and I press myself into the back of the chair. It's even more uncomfortable.

President Nowell closes the folder and hands it over. "You're overreacting, Jacob."

"Maybe. Let's just have a look." He looks at the papers.

I feel sick. I don't want him reading those words.

What will he think of me?

"Dr. Lee, I didn't…I didn't…"

"It's all right, Professor Jha. I'm sure there are explanations."

I sit on the high stool at the kitchen peninsula. I'm doing a crossword as Dadi brushes and braids my hair. She asks what ribbon I want—red or blue plaid.

"Journey."

"What is that, dear one?" she asks.

"Traveling from one place to another. Journey." I write the letters in the squares.

"Ah." Dadi picks up a ribbon. "I will do the blue plaid. Will that be alright with you?"

"Yes." She ties it to the bottom of my braid.

"There. You look lovely." Her voice is soft—wind in the bamboo.

Sierra's voice is not soft. She sits at the dining room

table with Baba. They are talking loudly about money. I forget my crossword and stare at them.

Sierra grips the edge of the table. "She needs a special school!"

"Yes. We agree, but we will not just hand you money. Find the school and we'll deal directly with them."

"I need money to get around...to look...to find something."

Baba shakes his head. "*Not* five hundred dollars."

"Then two. I can get started with two. I'll...I'll look around and get back to you."

Baba reaches out for Sierra's hands. "Shreya, come home."

Sierra snatches her hands away. "Don't call me that!"

"But that is your name precious one, and your family is the most important thing. You and Paige need to come home."

"We have a home!" Sierra yells.

Dadi moves to sit at the table. "But your piano is here. Your violin is here. When was the last time you played the piano?"

Sierra moans then slams her fist on the table.

I cover my ears.

"Stop trying to run my life!"

Baba's voice is louder. "Then stop trying to ruin your life! And Paige's life!"

Ganesha watches as I tear my crossword into little pieces.

"Paige?"

Dr. Lee is speaking to me.

"Paige?" He sits in the other uncomfortable green chair.

I look at him. "Yes?"

He leans towards me. "Can you tell me the story of the young man hugging you?"

I feel heat creeping up my neck. "He wasn't hugging me. He was helping me."

"What do you mean?"

"I was caught in the center of the protest. There was yelling and spitting, and people were all around me."

Dr. Lee nods. "Which is difficult for you."

"I couldn't breathe."

"So, what happened?"

Heat spreads across my face. "Mr. Kimball came up behind me and held me tight."

"And that kind of hug is a therapy when you're having an episode, right?"

"Yes. He pulled me out of the crowd."

"And how did he know that hug would help you?"

"He said he studied about it."

Dr. Lee stands and looks at President Nowell. "So, here we have a situation where a student admirably aids a teacher, yet you're believing the lies of a disgruntled student who has previously sent you false reports."

"Not false."

"Okay, over inflated."

"I have to follow up on every accusation, Jacob."

Dr. Lee throws my file on the desk. "Then start by questioning the liar."

"What about the assault?"

"Really, Marcus? Again, reported by the same liar. If I were you, I'd be looking into a possible vendetta against a teacher."

He smiles down at me. "Come on, Professor Jha. We have classes to teach."

I stand from the uncomfortable chair and follow the Chinese Dragon out of the room.

Fifteen

I STAND AT THE PICTURE WINDOW flipping through the fan chart. "It might be Star Gazer or Silken Peacock." I flip to another strip. "Maybe—Skyfall." I like looking through the colors, it calms me. I hear the patio door scrape open and Baba stamping his feet before he enters. A trickle of cold seeps in and curls around my bare feet. The patio door closes, and Baba comes in and hangs his jacket.

"What are you doing?"

"Finding the color of the water."

He raises his eyebrows. "I see. And still in your pajamas?"

I don't answer him.

He goes to the kitchen and gets a glass of water. "I'm going to the hardware store later. Come with me."

"No. No, thank you."

"I think you should shower and get dressed."

I hold the fan chart to the window. "Maybe Crystal Stream."

"Paige."

"Yes?"

"What are you thinking?"

"I'm trying to figure out the color of the water today."

"Why?"

"Because…because…I…"

He persists. " What's on your mind?

I'm quiet, looking at the colors. "After the winter break, I'm thinking of not returning."

"To your teaching job?"

"Yes."

Baba is quiet for a long time. I glance at him, and he shakes his head. "You realize everything Dr. Lee said in your meeting with the President is true."

"I don't know what that means, Baba?"

"None of those accusations had any validity. When Jacob spoke to me, he was furious that President Nowell had even called you in."

"Hmm." I feel pressure at the back of my eyes as I think back to the green chair and the President shuffling papers. "Do we need to talk about this?"

"I think we do." Baba sets down his glass of water and sighs. "Don't let harsh comments by a couple of malcontent students make you give up something you love."

I lean my forehead against the cool window. "But President Nowell said I was out of my depth. That perhaps this is something I can't navigate."

"I assure you, he wasn't speaking about your teaching ability," Baba says softly. He sits at the table and motions to me. "Come and sit Paige."

"I don't feel like doing that."

"I know, but for me?"

I hesitate, then I lay the fan chart on the table and sit. "I could work with Dr. Williamson on string theory. I could write a book comparing Confucianism and the writings of C.S. Lewis."

"Of course, you could. There are a dozen things you could do and do well, Paige, but what do you *want* to do?"

Ganesha sits on my bed comfortably snuggled into our pillow. I sit in front of him showing him the pictures of the book and reading the story of the demon and the elephant. He doesn't like it and begins to trumpet.

"Hush, little god. It turns out alright in the end." I show him the picture of the elephant pack being caught in the monsoon rains. "And the lead elephant stamped, and the mother elephants called out for help, and the baby elephant cried. But the demon in the rain only laughed and beat upon them." I turn the page to show the demon in the rain.

Ganesha weeps.

"Now, there's nothing to cry about, Ganesha. I told you it will be alright in the end."

He trumpets at me and asks me what I know. I'm only five. He has lived for eternity and has seen many sad stories of life that haven't turned out well. I don't know what he means. I flip to the final pages of the book. The baby elephant has found a place for the pack to shelter until the storm passes. And, on the last page the sun is shining, and the baby elephant is throwing red dirt into the air and laughing.

"See, Ganesha. The sun is shining."
Ganesha shakes his head and his ears flap.
Does he believe me?

"I want to teach, Baba, but I don't know how." A single tear escapes my eye.

"You do know how, Professor Jha. I love your lessons when you go over them with me. He puts his palms together in the namaste prayer. Believe me, Dear One, you do a good job. Mr. Kimball says the students in your physics class think you're terrific."

"Not all."

"You are never going to get a hundred percent of your students to like you, Paige. It doesn't happen." He chuckles. "Well, maybe in theater classes."

That would have been funny in different circumstances but today another tear rolls down my cheek. I take the fan chart back to the window. "I think it will be less painful if I stop now."

Baba stands and leaves the room.

I am left alone with my embarrassment. I look at the chart for more colors. After a few minutes I hear him reenter the dining room.

"Paige, I have something for you."

I turn and see Ganesha. It is him. His left ear a bit droopy where my young hand pulled it; the tummy threadbare from being my pillow. I drop the fan chart and reach for him. "How?"

My feet won't move so Baba walks him to me.

"How, Baba? Where did you find him?"

"Sierra brought him."

"My Sierra? When?"

"A few months ago."

I look down at my treasured friend, my mind—confused. "Why didn't I see her?"

"You were teaching. She brought him by, but she wouldn't stay."

"How did she find him?" I look up at him for answers.

Baba shakes his head. "She wasn't making sense, Paige. She was high on something and babbling about your old house and getting him out of the floorboards. I don't think she knew…"

My heart jumps. "Wait! Wait, Baba! She got him out of the floorboards?"

"That's what she said. I'm sure the drugs were talking."

I stare at Ganesha. "No, Baba. No. She got him out of the floor of our house. There was this secret space." I look straight at my grandfather. "Sierra was *there*—the day they wrecked our house. I saw her! She was there! She went there to get Ganesha. I yelled to the workers that I saw her inside and they stopped…for one minute they stopped."

It's hard to breathe. "If I hadn't yelled…if they hadn't stopped…"

Baba stares at me in disbelief, then sits heavily in one of the chairs.

I take Ganesha to look at the color of the water. Tears

wet his head as I smack my hand on the window, again and again and again, sending atoms dancing through the glass. "Why did you wait so long to tell me this Baba? To give Ganesha back to me?"

"I didn't want you to know that Sierra had come."

"Why?"

"Because I didn't want you to be reminded of all the chaos and pain. You have enough to deal with."

"That's not for you to say, Baba. You must stop treating me like I'm twelve."

"Wait! Wait, now. Is that fair? I have always encouraged your independence, but in your relationship with Sierra, I'm protective of you."

"Where is she now?"

"I don't know."

I turn and stare at him.

"Really, Paige. I don't know. I asked her where she was living, but she wouldn't tell me. She wouldn't even come into the house. She handed me Ganesha, told me to give him to you, and left."

I turn back to the window. "Where is she, Baba? Why didn't she stay to see me? Seven years and she doesn't come to see me? Seven years? Where is she?"

"I think she's lost, Little Twig."

A growl grumbles in my chest, and it hurts. "Lost, like Ganesha."

We stand on the hard wet sand and watch the ripples

of water creep to our toes. I look at Sierra's face and see a smile. We have just started my chart of human emotions and I know that this face means happy.

"Are you happy?"

"I suppose...at the moment." She tucks errant wisps of hair behind her ears and gazes out at the ocean.

A minute of **peace for us.**

"I don't want her to be lost, Baba. I want her to have a minute of peace."

"We would all like that." He walks over to me and gives my braid a gentle tug. "And I pray for *you* to have a minute of peace."

We stand together silently as I dry my eyes on Ganesha's tummy.

Finally, Baba's voice comes to me. "Paige, you must think again about teaching. I know you and giving it up would make you feel empty. A box with nothing inside."

"An empty mandala."

"Yes."

"Hmm."

Baba takes my hand and I let him. "I think the color of the water is whatever you want to name it, Jaanu."

Beloved One – the Hindi name ripples through my heart.

I stare at the water. "So, you think I can choose?"

"I do." He roughs the top of Ganesha's head. "And here's another thing I think."

"What?"

"I think that you should come with me to the hardware store."

"Why?"

"Because then you'd have to shower and get dressed."

"Hmm."

"I will buy you a wooden rake."

Ganesha and I contemplate his offer.

Sixteen

I WEAR THE OUTFIT Elly gave me for my birthday. My hair, out of its braid, falls loose around my face and down my back. Baba said I should start the new term with a fresh perspective, but as I pull papers from my satchel and set out my computer, I feel I'm on display in a department store window. I know the students are considering my new look and I have the urge to click my pen. Instead, I lay it aside and finish preparation for class. There is a palpable energy in the room as the students chat and laugh. I want to absorb their sense of abandon.

I pull my hair into a circle comb, and let it fall. It is not my braid, but it seems more familiar than loose about my face. I begin the power point with an image of Buddha. The class quiets.

"Good morning, students. I hope you all had a restful break?"

This question is answered with murmurs of assent.

"Looks like *you* had a good break, Professor Jha," Miss Aston offers.

"And why is that, Miss Aston?"

"It's just that we like the new look." Another murmur of assent from the class members.

"Ah. I see. 'Fashion is the armor to survive the reality of everyday life.' That from designer Bill Cunningham."

The class laughs.

"I'd hate to come up against you in a game of Trivial Pursuit," someone calls out.

"So true," Miss Aston responds. "Really, is there anything you don't know about, Professor?"

"Cooking."

The class laughs again.

"It's good to be back, Professor Jha," Miss Aston says.

"I hope you feel the same when I return your papers from last term."

The class groans.

"Actually, you did well." I pick up the remote to the computer. "Now, shall we get to work?" They ready their laptops and notebooks and I feel a settling of mind—an ability to breathe. I move through several images of the Buddha. "We see statues of Buddha at rest, in meditation, solemn, happy, sleeping, sitting under a tree, holding a lotus blossom—in stone, in gold, and the list goes on. There is Buddha statuary unique to India which differs from China, which differs then again with Japan." I bring up an image of an Asian sage. "We finished last term with a discussion of Siddhartha Gautama, who was an Indian prince before his enlightenment."

"Is that actually a painting of him, Professor?"

"Probably not. Just a representation. His life is mostly legend; therefore, no one knows what Siddhartha Gautama looked like."

"Too bad there weren't selfies back in the day," a student says.

"I doubt Buddha would have owned a cell phone."

The class laughs and I wonder what I said that was funny.

"The next few classes we'll study Buddhist philosophy. Now, you should have read Chapter Seven of *Looking into the Sun* during break. I bring up another image. "Here we find the Enlightenment of Buddha as he sits fasting under the bodhi tree."

I turn to them. "So, who can tell me the first Noble Truth of the Enlightenment?" I'm surprised when Miss Fennimore raises her hand. "Yes, Miss Fennimore?"

"Life is suffering."

"Exactly. Life is suffering. Some translations say stressful or unable to satisfy, but I think suffering is the best definition. The Sanskrit word for this is dukkha."

Sierra and I sit on my bedroom floor, in the corner, facing the wall. I have duct tape over my mouth and Sierra has her head on her bent knees. The front door slams and we jump. The house grows still. Sierra lifts her head and looks at me. I turn to the corner.

"Here. Come here," she says flatly. She reaches for my face and I back away. "I'm so sorry. I should have stopped him." She scoots towards me. "Here, let me get that off." She secures an edge of the tape and tugs.

I whimper.

"Sorry. Sorry, Paige."

Tears flow down her cheeks.

"So sorry."

She rips it off quickly and I cry out.

I look at the expectant faces of my students. "And the second Noble Truth?" Miss Fennimore's hand again. "Yes, Miss Fennimore?"

"There's a purpose in suffering." Her voice is soft but constricted.

"Yes. Dukkha has a purpose."

Miss Aston's hand raises but she speaks before I have a chance to call on her.

"I don't understand this, Professor." Her voice has an uncharacteristic edge. "How can suffering have a purpose? Buddha sits under a tree, not eating for forty days, gains enlightenment, and suffering is his first Noble Truth? I don't get it. I hate suffering."

"Of course." I come around in front of the podium. "How many agree with Miss Aston?"

Everyone raises their hand, or nods. "Now, how many have suffered?"

In slow increments the hands go up again. I include mine at the end. "Buddha discovered that everyone suffers, and when we understand the cause of dukkha, which is the third Noble Truth, we can be liberated from unprofitable cravings, stress, and selfishness."

I look at Miss Fennimore. "Kim, would you like to bookend the teaching of the great sage? What is the fourth Noble Truth?"

She looks at me; suffering etched on her face. "We must step onto the enlightened path: meditation, mindfulness, living a life that benefits others."

"Yes. The Christian sage Jesus taught the same—to find your life, you must give up your life." I bring up an image of Buddha sitting in a celestial realm. "So, Miss Aston, according to Buddha's enlightenment, what is Nirvana?"

"It's something like a permanent heaven when you don't have to be reincarnated anymore to learn truth."

"Yes. Nirvana means 'the putting out of fire.' The fire of self or selfishness. This is a noble goal." The next image is one of the Happy Buddha, chubby with a wide smile on his face. "In honor of the Happy Buddha, I will give you the rest of the class to start on your self-evaluation assignment."

The class claps.

I put my palms together and give them a little bow. "Namaste," I say. "I see your soul."

"Namaste," they return.

As I'm shutting down my computer, Miss Fennimore approaches the desk. I feel my heart quicken and I take a breath.

"Professor Jha?"

"Yes?"

"I was wondering if we could meet sometime?"

I put papers into my bag. "I have an office hour at four pm today. Will that work?"

"Yeah. That'll be good."

I glance at her as she goes back to her seat. She doesn't sit but gathers her belongings and slowly ascends the stairs to exit.

"Namaste," I say quietly so only my heart hears.

It is 4:10 and Miss Fennimore has not arrived. I'm drinking ginger ale and attempting to read an article by Dr. Witten on M Theory. My attention is dragged to dust particles in the air, a picture of me warily holding Yash Jha, my row of books—one out of sequence. I stand to fix the issue when there's a soft tap on the door.

"Come in."

The door opens and Miss Fennimore enters. "Sorry I'm late, Professor. I had a…"

"No trouble. Only eleven minutes. Have a seat."

We sit at the same time. I try to see myself as her teacher and her my student, but we're peers—at least in age. I straighten the papers on my desk.

Listen Paige, you're always going to be different. Your mind is like Lucy in the Sky with Diamonds. Most people are average…

"I need to apologize to you, Professor Jha."

Unexpected.

My fingers stop organizing the papers.

"For reporting you to President Nowell. I didn't want to complain about you, but some of my friends said I should."

"Hmm."

"In fact, they said I had to. That you needed to be cut down to size."

"I don't know what that means."

"You know—put in your place."

I still don't know what her words mean, but I nod. "I see."

She hangs her head. "I didn't want to get you into trouble. I'm sorry."

"I'm glad you came to see me, Kim. I accept your apology."

She looks up. "Really? Just like that?"

Her bangs nearly poke into her eyes, and my fingers itch to brush them to the side, instead I nod. "Those who cannot forgive others break the bridge over which they themselves must pass."

"Buddha?"

"Confucius."

A weak smile touches the corner of her mouth. "I knew it had to be one of those guys." She stands and sways slightly. "Ah…thank you, Professor Jha. Thank you so much. I won't take up anymore of your time." She sways again and all the color drains from her face. She sits.

"Miss Fennimore, are you ill?"

"Pregnant."

"What?"

"Pregnant." She looks at me, but I cannot verify what her features are telling me. There is no emotion like this on my chart.

"Can I have some water, Professor?"

I go to my mini fridge and get her a bottle of water. "Are you tired?"

She has a difficult time cracking the plastic lid on the bottle. Tears start. "So tired."

I glance at the photo of me and Yash Jha. "How far along are you?"

"Two months."

"Hmm."

"Everyone around me says I should get an abortion…"

I cover my ears. There is the sensation of warm dry washcloths and the sound of words like rats trying to gnaw through the fabric.

You should have just had an abortion. You should have just had an abortion. You should have just had an abortion.

"No. Stop."

"Sorry, Professor. I don't know why I'm telling you about this. I didn't mean to upset you."

I drop my hands away from my ears and sit. "I mean, don't."

She brushes tears from her cheeks. "What?"

I force myself to look at her. "Your baby needs to live, Kim."

New tears. "I heard its heartbeat…on an ultrasound."

"Sound waves with frequencies higher than the upper audible limit of human hearing."

"It wasn't what I expected. I...I..." She looks straight at me with that face of suffering.

I blink.

"I don't know what to do, Professor. I don't know what to do."

"You heard a heartbeat."

"I did!" she wails.

I push back into my chair and feel atoms hitting my face. *You're like Lucy in the Sky with Diamonds.*

I tap my fingers on the arms of my chair. "Faced with what is right, to leave it undone shows a lack of courage."

Silence.

She nods. "Confucius again?"

"Hmm."

She takes a drink of water and I see color returning to her face. "All those protests and it comes down to this. All that yelling and screaming about something I didn't know anything about."

My phone rings and Miss Fennimore stands abruptly. "I'd better get going."

"Hello, Baba. Can you wait a moment?"

Kim is shouldering her backpack and wiping tears on the sleeve of her sweatshirt.

"Thank you, Professor Jha. Thanks for accepting my apology and...for understanding."

"Don't forget your water."

"Oh yeah, thanks."

She grabs the bottle and I walk her to the door. "Kim?"

"Yeah?"

"We can talk again, if you'd like?"

She hesitates. "Really?"

"Of course. Yes."

"Thanks."

I open the door and she's gone. I pick up my phone. "Baba, are you there?" I attempt to calm my heartbeat as I listen to his words. He asks if I need a ride home. A storm's about to break. "I'll be fine. I'm leaving now and the bus stop is close." He tells me to be careful. I put my phone in my pocket and gather my belongings. My hands shake and I lay them flat on my desk and press down.

I pray Kim's baby will cure cancer or fly to Saturn or play the piano. I pray Kim's baby will survive.

The wind is my enemy. It presses against my body and I long to set down my satchel and computer bag. *No*, I tell myself, because I'd only have to pick them up again. The bus stop is three blocks and I hope to get there before it rains. It's dark at five pm. A gust of wind pushes against me.

His pacing never stops—his agitation. I'm eight and I reach for his hand, but there are no fingers, only fists. He moves into the crowd of angry people. I press against Sierra as we shiver in the November rain. Finn shouts to the group about the corruption in the banking system. The evil of capitalist greed. The crowd shouts loudly and I cover my ears. Everyone shouts about the evil bankers. Voices locked in horrible noise.

Someone throws a beer bottle, and a police officer drops to the ground, blood spurting from his temple. Everyone surges forward except me and Sierra. I try to read the expression on her face. The rain has washed it away. Her eyelids droop as though she wants to sleep. Another angry shout and I hide behind Sierra's satchel. I'm cold. Isn't everyone else cold? Sierra latches onto the back of my jacket and drags me into a storefront alcove. I cover my ears and stamp my feet.

A crack of thunder and my heart pounds.

I should have let Baba pick me up.

I walk faster. This is the lonely part of the trek—no houses on either side of the street, no campus lighting. A few drops of rain hit my face, and from behind me I hear movement. I turn. Three figures in black clothing are coming toward me. I turn back and continue walking at a faster pace. Their footsteps mimic mine. My thoughts begin to fracture.

"Hey! Professor Jha!" a voice calls.

I stop.

Some of my students.

I breathe and turn around.

"You're late tonight," says another. "We've been waiting for you."

"I had a meeting with a student."

"Poor student."

Now the threesome is close enough for me to see their faces. One, I recognize. "Kennedy?"

"Hi, Paige."

"Miss Everett, I would prefer you not call me…"

"I don't really care what you prefer," she snarls.

I step back. "I need to catch the bus." I start to move away and she grabs the strap of my satchel.

She screams, "My dad took away my car because of you!"

I try to make sense of this. "I don't see how I…"

"He didn't like that I reported you to President Nowell. Turns out my dear deluded dad is one of your fans. Makes me puke. Worst teacher on campus and he stands up for you. Won't stand up for me, but you? You?" she's still screaming.

I cover my ears and step back. "I need to get to the bus."

She lunges at me. "You're pathetic!" She rips my hands away from my ears and shoves me.

"Hey!" her male friend protests. "No rough stuff."

"Pathetic." She shoves me again. "Always looking down on people because you're so freakishly smart? Test and measure."

Shove.

"Test and measure."

Shove.

Her other friend grabs her wrist. "Cut it out, Kennedy! Have you snapped or something? She's a teacher."

"She's a freak!"

Her male friend grabs her other arm. "Let's get out of here!"

Miss Everett breaks free from their grip and charges me. She stumbles; the law of physics propels her forward. She slams into me, and I fall.

Seventeen

S ATURN AND THE GHOST NEBULA *swirl past in the vacuum of space. Lao Tzu walks with me on The Way while Ganesha places a string of orange flowers around my neck. I smell warm ghee and cumin while Dadi taps the time on the arm of her chair. Piano music—Chopin. A wooden rake and yellow leaves. Rain.*

Sierra teaches me the alphabet. Soap bubbles float around the sun. Kali, goddess of destruction, stands by the window looking at the dark sky. Demons in black hoods put their hands on me. Rain.

Sierra pushes me under the bed. I'm twelve and even though my body is thin, I don't fit as well as I did when I was eight. Finn grabs Ganesha and hisses at me that I'm too old to have a toy. What would the cops think? He disappears.

I scream and Sierra tells me to click my pen—that she'll be back and bring Ganesha. She promises to come back. She promises.

She doesn't come.

Police sirens scream in the distance. I click my pen. I hear

Finn cursing. The leopard is in the cage. Sierra screams at me to stay under the bed as Finn grabs her wrist and drags her towards the back door. They leave me. They leave me alone. Now the flashing lights are at our house. They slice through my skin like razors.

Climbing. My keds on the flagstone steps. Surya Deul—temple of the sun. Lord Vishnu—blue skin, crown of cobras protects the porch and the porch swing.

"Welcome, Paige Jha," my grandfather says, in a voice like waves on the Bay of Bengal.

"Namaste," I say, in a voice like the stillness of a shallow pond.

I wake.

I see my grandfather's face. The visage is blurry, and I close my eyes.

"Dear one, open your eyes. Can you open them?" He speaks to someone, and a voice speaks back. They are far away.

I am walking on the ocean. I have discovered the science of compressing water molecules to form a pathway over the deep. The Great Maker of the Universe knows the ocean. He knows the water. He knows the molecules.

The woman in the dark pantsuit keeps trying to take my arm. I pull away. She asks me where my parents are. I don't understand her question. Slivers of thought tumble. What is your name? Paige Jha. Do you have any family nearby? Marine View Drive Federal Way. What is their name? Baba and Dadi. Oh, but Dadi is dead now, so it's just Baba. She asks more questions, but I have finished talking. I dig the toe of my tennis shoe into the dirt and press my back against the police car. My pen is in my pocket. I click it until a policeman in a uniform takes it away. I close my eyes and put my hands over my ears. My feet stamp.

Someone tugs at my eyelid and there's a flash of light.
"Paige? Paige, open your eyes."
I do. Everything is fuzzy. I blink several times.
"Do you know where you are?"
I don't.

"I'm going to sit you up a bit more." The back of my bed rises.

It's never done that before.

A stab of pain shoots into my head and I vomit. The movement of the bed stops, and I'm surrounded by people and voices. My hands begin to shake, and I can't breathe.
"I'm here, Paige. I'm right here with you." Baba takes my hand. "Breathe, Jaanu."
You're going to be alright."
I think I might die.

There is a warm blue light. Am I looking at the water from the dining room window? I rub my fingers on the sheet. Where are my fingertips? The blue light fades and my eyes open a slit. I hear the click of a machine and feel something in my nose. Light coming through a window. Elly's face.

"Nrsberaeyesropen."

I don't know that language. I close my eyes, but someone pinches the back of my hand, and they open again. A woman's face. Not Elly.

"Miss Jha, can you understand me?"

I try to say yes, but the word sticks in my…I can't remember the word. I want to see Elly's face. Where did she go? I close my eyes and search for the warm blue light.

I stand inside a mandala. Bright. Colorful. Circular pathways leading to a center. I look right then left. Which way to go? A voice answers that it doesn't matter. It's a circle—just begin walking. All truth can be circumscribed. I walk and the world spins—the bright light dims.

Someone is squeezing my arm. I open my eyes.

"Uncle?"

Aakesh stares at me. "Paige?" He says my name as though he's just remembered it.

"Hmm."

"Are you awake?"

I don't know what this means. His face disappears.

What is this place? I'm sitting part way up. *My bed doesn't do this.*

I try to focus on the unfamiliar room and my vision slides. I panic as I feel a blockage in my nose. My fingers shake as they try and pull it out.

Why is there plastic in my nose…and around my ears? Mewling sounds are trapped in my throat as I grab at the tubing. Baba and a woman are at my side.

"Paige, it's alright. It's oxygen. You need that," Baba says.

"Here, let me help you," the woman says. She takes the tubing and slips it back into my nose. I pull it out. "The doctor is on his way, and you really need to keep this in."

"Maybe we can give her a little break," Baba says in his most soothing voice. "She's never been a patient in a hospital."

The woman nods. She lays her hand on my arm. "Paige, you need to calm down. It's going to be alright." She looks at Baba. "But when the doctor comes, he'll decide about the oxygen."

"Of course."

There is a bell. The woman turns quickly, and her face disappears.

"Baba?" My voice is raspy and it hurts to talk.

"Would you like some ice chips?"

I don't know what this means, but I nod.

He brings over a white plastic cup and feeds me ice chips with a plastic spoon. "Let them melt slowly."

We are like this for a space of time—him feeding me ice chips, me—confused.

"Am I in a hospital, Baba?"

He nods.

"Why?"

He sets the cup aside and takes my hand. I let him. "You were injured, dear one." His eyes fill with tears. "You fell… cement curbing…" He weeps. "I can't talk about this, Little Twig."

"Fell?" I think of rain and hands pushing me. "But…"

"We don't need to talk about this now." He gets out his handkerchief and wipes his face.

"How long have I been here?"

"This is the beginning of the fourth day."

Four days?

"Will I die?"

Baba pats my hand. "Of course not. And you are speaking." He looks to the ceiling and takes a deep breath.

"Baba?"

He focuses on my face. "How are you feeling?"

A difficult question. "In my body?"

"Yes."

"I feel dizzy and…" I pause to think of the word. "Nauseous."

His tears come again. "I'm so sorry, dear one."

A man with white hair and a white coat comes to Baba's side and pats him on his shoulder. "But here she is, Avi, with her eyes open and speaking actual words!"

"Yes, that's true, Robert."

The doctor smiles at me and I look at my hand. More tubing.

"Miss Jha, I'm Dr. Penn and I am very glad to see you with your eyes open." He turns to Baba. "Avi, I'm going to give her an extensive examination, so if you could just go to the waiting room?"

Baba stands with a frown on his face. "But we have been waiting and waiting for her to wake up."

"I know. I understand. Just a little longer and I'll let you come and pester her."

"Please tell me good news."

"Isn't that what you've been praying for?"

"Yes."

"Then leave it in His hands."

Baba turns to go. I reach for him. "But I…"

"The doctor will take good care of you, Paige. He will find out how you're doing and then your family can come see you." His face has two expressions, his mouth gives me a small grin, but his eyes show pain. He goes and I feel tired.

The doctor smiles at me. "Now, let's see if we can get you up and dancing."

"I don't dance."

Dr. Penn chuckles. "I would be grateful for sitting and not vomiting. Shall we try?"

I nod and he reaches to take my hand.

I let him.

Eighteen

BABA AND I STAND on the hard sand and let the waves come to our bare toes. Baba is on my left side because I still have weakness in that leg.

One minute of peace.

A cold wave covers our feet.

"I haven't done this in years," Baba says, a smile in his voice.

"It's nice, isn't it?"

He gives me a side hug. "Warm for March."

"Unseasonably. 60 degrees Fahrenheit—15.555 degrees Celsius."

He gives me another hug and clears his throat. "My calculator is back!"

"Broken for a time."

Baba clears his throat again. "But I'm only going to think of your progress. Only a month out from the hospital and look at you."

"Dr. Penn is pleased."

"As he should be, Paige. You've been tenacious about your physical therapy."

"Hmm."

Sierra rummages in the hall closet bringing out poster paper, scissors, and paint. It's Finn's property and we're not supposed to touch it. Some of the papers have red scars of paint.

"Let's make a mess. What do you say?"

I don't like mess.

Sierra throws back the shabby area rug and drops the stuff onto the floor. "Let's make a mess! Let's paint every-thing! We don't even care if it gets on the floor!" She's talking fast like the lady at the welfare office. "We'll show that pig he can't hurt us and get away with it." She sits and picks up the scissors. "Sit down, Paige. Sit with me. Sit."

Ganesha and I sit. She hands me the scissors. My sev-en-year-old hand drops them. "Never mind, never mind. I'll teach you." She puts them in my hand and corrects where my fingers go. "See, they're not too big. Just a little bigger than yours. So, practice. Cut this paper. Cut, cut, cut! Cut it all up."

I practice cutting the paper as Sierra talks and curses and covers the paper with angry words.

"Baba?"

"Yes?"

"This morning, I overheard you and Aakesh talking about my student, Kennedy."

Baba stiffens. "Yes, but she's not your student anymore."

"Expelled?"

"Of course. And I hope she goes to jail for a while." His voice is abrasive and tired.

"Hmm."

We're silent as the waves ripple in.

"Baba?"

"Yes?"

"When I climbed the steps to your house when I was twelve…"

He groans. "Why are you remembering this, Jaanu? On such a beautiful day let's put that aside."

"No, Baba. I need to talk about it." A larger wave threatens our feet, and we step back. Still the icy water comes to our ankles.

"I would prefer not to remember, dear one."

I grasp the sleeve of his jacket. "I need to know, Baba! I need to know about the day the lady in the black suit brought me to your house." My throat burns like I drank ocean water. "Did Finn kill someone?"

Baba is a long time answering. "Finn, threw a brick at a young man at the rally."

"What? Why?"

"The boy had a different opinion." Baba's voice is husky. "Eighteen years old—paralyzed."

My hands are ice. "Oh Baba." My throat tightens and tears come from the corners of my eyes. Another wave covers my feet. "Younger than me."

Baba is silent.

Cold water swirls around my ankles. "And Finn went to prison."

"Fifteen years."

Here Paige, I'm putting these glow stars and planets on your ceiling. They are magic. They'll keep away the shadows.

The frothy water is like the Ghost Nebula. I lose my balance and Baba steadies me.

"And Sierra? Where did she go that night?"

Baba shakes his head and sighs. "After all these years are you sure you want to know?"

I clench my fists. "Yes."

"Psychiatric lockdown."

The molecules shatter. I grip the sleeve of Baba's jacket, so I don't fall. "I hate them! I hate them!" My words chock me. "Why wasn't I good enough for them? Why, Baba? I wanted to be their cause. Why wasn't I their cause? I wanted my mother to love me." I rush out into the ocean. I don't want to walk on it, I want it to cover me. I hear the frantic voice of my grandfather calling me, but I only want the sound of the ocean. I don't understand a drop of this churning water. I am waist deep and the water is freezing. My limbs stiffen and my breath seizes. As I struggle through the waves, the cold pounds in my head, but still, I hear a voice. It's Baba shouting the words of Gandhi.

"When I despair, I remember that all through history the ways of truth and love have always won!" His words reach me. I know *these* words. I stop. Waves continue to crash against me—more words come…

"There have been tyrants and murderers, and for a time they can seem invincible…"

Cold salty water slaps my face and I choke. "… but in the end…" I turn back. "…they always fall."

I'm washed into my Baba's arms. "Think of it—always."

Nineteen

I TURN THE KEY in the lock, place my hand on the door-knob, and open the door. I count to four and enter. I smell garlic and ginger and spices. Grandfather is cooking Tandoori Chicken. I place my keys in the blue ceramic bowl on the entry way table, my book bag on the wall peg, and my briefcase on the floor by the umbrella stand. I straighten the get-well cards from my students. I adjust the picture of Dadi and say good evening to her. I know I will find her in heaven.

I am the way, the truth, and the life.

"Are you home, Professor Jha?" Baba calls from the kitchen.

"I'm home, Baba." I hear a murmur of voices as I approach the kitchen. I enter to find Aakesh and Elly sitting at the dining room table with Mr. Kimball. He is gathering books and papers into his backpack.

I frown. "Are you here again?"

Aakesh shakes his head. "Remember what I told you, Donavan. All sorts of weird stuff just flies out of her mouth."

"Nonsense," I say as I go to lift Yash out of his playpen. I take him to the window to look at the color of the water. He slaps his hand on the glass sending atoms rippling. "It's just that he's transferred colleges, so I don't know why he still comes here for tutoring."

"Oh, for heaven's sake, Professor Jha," Baba says as he puts Pakora into a pan of sizzling oil. "You're a genius and you can't figure that out?"

Aakesh and Elly roar with laughter and I take a step back. I glance at Mr. Kimball and see a wide grin. He winks at me, and I feel heat come into my face.

"Nonsense." In a fluster I hand the baby to Elly and go get the silverware. "Clear up that stuff so I can set the table."

Now everyone but me and baby Yash are laughing. Through the clamor I hear notes from our piano; halting, jumbled, an attempt at Chopin's *Prelude 7 in A Major*.

"Hush," Baba says as he turns off the stove. "Hush." As everyone quiets, we all hear the uncertain notes.

"Baba, who's playing our piano?" He and I go into the hallway where we find the front door open.

"I must not have secured it." I shut the door as Baba steps into the living room. I join him.

"It's her piano too," Baba says, his voice wrapped in tenderness.

Sierra's thin fingers move across the keys. I stare at her. Bare feet, Levi's, flannel shirt. Dadi would not be pleased with her posture—bent and unsure. Another wrong note. I turn and move out of the room. Baba tries to stop me, but I pull my arm away. The notes follow me, thrumming into my brain. I snatch Ganesha off my bedroom dresser and go back. I push past the others at the front room entry to find Baba still standing rooted in place; tears the only movement. It's as though he's holding his breath, praying the apparition won't vanish. Sierra keeps playing as though the world is far away.

I set Ganesha on the piano and sit. The fingers stop moving.

"You have to play to the end," I whisper.

I put my fingers on the keys and begin where she stopped. We play Chopin together. We play to the end.

The End

ABOUT THE AUTHOR

GALE SEARS is an award-winning author, known for her historical accuracy and intensive research. Gale received a BA in playwriting from Brigham Young University and a master's degree in theater arts from the University of Minnesota. She is the author of the bestselling *The Silence of God* and *Letters in the Jade Dragon Box*. She and her husband George are the parents of two children and reside in Salt Lake City, Utah.